"Your, um
Sam said,

"Oh." Tabitha's hand flew to the front panel of her Levi's. "They're too tight," she explained, tugging at the hem of her shirt, "because of the baby."

Sam's eyes jerked up to meet hers, then darted back to her stomach. A goofy, slightly awed grin tugged at his lips. Without looking away from her belly, he moved closer. "The baby," he said, almost to himself.

His reaction warmed her. "Yeah, I know," she murmured. Wanting to share this miracle with him, she took his hand in both of hers and placed it on the gentle swell of her stomach.

But to her surprise, he slipped his hand lower, going under the hem of her shirt. His fingertips, surprisingly rough, eased into the V made by her parted jeans and his thumb rested on her belly button.

Desire raced through her, sending shivers radiating through her body. Suddenly she felt as if she couldn't breathe. She closed her eyes, hoping to gain some control. But when she opened them again, she found him staring intently at her....

Then he kissed her....

Dear Reader,

I can't tell you how thrilled I am to be writing for
Harlequin Temptation, the series I've been reading
since its launch (yes, I started young) and the line
that so many of my favorite authors still write for.

And I'm especially thrilled to make my debut with
this story. *Baby, Be Mine* is very special to me, not
only because it's my first book and it's set in my
hometown of Austin, Texas, but also because it
contains several elements from one of my favorite
stories—*Cyrano de Bergerac.* Who can resist a man
who loves a woman so strongly he's willing to help
another win her heart because he believes it will
make her happy? Add an unexpected pregnancy and
an outrageous radio contest and you know Sam and
Tabitha have a rocky road ahead of them.

I hope you enjoy reading this story as much
as I enjoyed writing it. If you'd like to hear about
my upcoming books, please visit my Web site,
www.EmilyMcKay.com. You can write me at
P.O. Box 163104, Austin, TX 78716-3104. I'd love
to hear from you!

Enjoy,

Emily McKay

Baby, Be Mine
Emily McKay

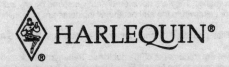

HARLEQUIN®

TORONTO • NEW YORK • LONDON
AMSTERDAM • PARIS • SYDNEY • HAMBURG
STOCKHOLM • ATHENS • TOKYO • MILAN • MADRID
PRAGUE • WARSAW • BUDAPEST • AUCKLAND

For my Uncle Phil, the most incredible storyteller, and for Aunt Doris, the woman he loved all his life. Your stories and your marriage always inspired me.

ISBN 0-373-69112-2

BABY, BE MINE

Copyright © 2003 by Emily McKaskle.

This edition published by arrangement with Harlequin Books S.A.

® and TM are trademarks of the publisher. Trademarks indicated with ® are registered in the United States Patent and Trademark Office, the Canadian Trade Marks Office and in other countries.

Visit us at www.eHarlequin.com

Printed in U.S.A.

Prologue

"IT'S STRESS," Tabitha Talbot murmured to herself. "Just stress."

Clutching her purse to her chest, she leaned her head against the tile wall. A curl of near-black hair blocked her view of the tiny, one-stall room. She blew it out of the way with a sigh. The cleansing breath didn't loosen the knot in her stomach. Nothing would. Not until the requisite five-minute wait for the results of the test had passed and she knew for sure it really was stress.

She'd never missed a period, no matter how stressful her life. If living with her flaky mother for eighteen years hadn't been stressful enough, then nothing else was.

"Please, just let it be stress."

She stared at her watch. Five thirty-nine. The morning radio show she cohosted with Sam Stevens wouldn't go on the air for another twenty-one minutes. Knowing she had plenty of time didn't lessen her anxiety.

Okay, so taking a pregnancy test at work probably wasn't the smartest thing she'd ever done. But dread had been gnawing at her since she'd stopped at the all-night drugstore to buy the test on the way in. She had to know. Now. Not eight hours from now when she finally made it home. Now.

So she'd crept into the "executive" bathroom, locked the door and peed on the stick. And in approximately three minutes and forty seconds, she'd know if she was pregnant.

The seconds seemed to stretch endlessly, as if a lifetime could be lived in between the pulsing of her watch's second hand.

She let her eyes drift closed, simulating a calm she didn't feel. She tried breathing deeply, but the cloying smell of the bathroom air freshener sickened her.

"You'll be okay," she told herself. "Whatever happens, you'll be okay. You're a mature adult. You're in a stable, long-term relationship with a great guy."

Hmm. "Great guy" was a bit of an overstatement. Bob wasn't great so much as…steady.

He didn't make her pulse pound or her knees weaken. That was okay. She could live without wild-animal attraction. What worried her was that he didn't make her laugh. Didn't challenge her mind.

She wasn't a child. She was long past expecting all that from one man. And steady was much higher on her list of desirable traits than funny or brilliant or even sexy.

"Steady is good," she reminded herself to quell the sinking feeling in her gut. "Steady is what you want."

She'd been raised by a single mother. Her mother's boyfriends had meant well, but none of them had been around long enough to be considered father figures. Her biological father had been just as temporary.

Since long before she'd left for college at the age of eighteen, she'd had her life all planned out. College, career, financial stability, marriage, then—maybe—a child or two.

Yes, she was doing things a little out of order. And yes, she had doubts about Bob. But she wasn't going to let that get in the way of her ten-year plan—which now apparently was going to happen in five years.

The thought made her pulse quicken. She glanced at her watch. Two minutes and fourteen seconds to go.

Since talking to herself hadn't helped, she concentrated on the piped-in music. Naturally, the station always played its own music. She heard the last few notes of one her favorite songs, followed by the station jingle. Then she heard her own prerecorded voice.

"If you didn't catch the show yesterday, here's what you missed..."

"So, what you're saying," Sam's voice began, "is that you're trying to trap your boyfriend into marrying you."

"Of course not," the listener snapped, "he wants to get married—"

Sam cut her off. "Honey, no man wants to get married. Women want to get married. Men just want to get laid."

A few seconds of canned laughter segued into a commercial for a new restaurant. Now she blocked out that, as well. The clip from this morning's show hadn't distracted her at all. It had only reminded her of what she already knew.

The sexy, single guys—the guys like Sam—were commitment-phobes. Boys pretending to be men. Luckily, Bob was nothing like Sam.

She glanced at her watch. Thirteen seconds to go. She exhaled, then stood. She draped the strap of her mammoth leather bag over the door handle, ignoring it as it dropped with a thud, and flexed her fingers to loosen the convulsed muscles. In two steps she crossed to the vanity. For a moment she stared at herself in the mirror.

"Whatever happens, you'll be okay." She met her reflection's gaze and nodded before looking at the wand.

One window framed a single blue stripe, proof the test had worked. In the other, two blue lines formed an X.

She was pregnant.

Anger flashed through her. This wasn't fair. All her life

she'd been so careful, so responsible. And now this? Her future ruined by poor quality control at a latex factory!

She grabbed the wand, intending to hurl it across the tiny room. In her anger, she whacked her knuckles against the vanity. Pain seared through her hand.

"Ouch! Ouch-ouch-ouch, ouch-ouch!"

Still grasping the wand, she shook her hand to dispel the sting.

"Are you okay?"

The question came from behind her. Too close behind her.

Panicked, she whirled to find Sam filling the doorway.

"What are you doing in here?" she gasped.

"What's in your hand?"

Horrified, she looked down at the incriminating wand then thrust her hand behind her back. With forced nonchalance she said, "Nothing."

His eyes narrowed suspiciously. "Was that a thermometer?"

"No. Leave!" She watched in disbelief as he stepped into the room, shutting the door behind him.

"If you're running a fever, you should go home. We can cover for you." His annoying protective instincts were very much at odds with his flippant radio personality. Sometimes she just didn't know which was the real Sam. Today she would have preferred the flippant Sam.

"I'm not sick. How did you get in?"

"The door was open. Now let me see the thermometer." He held out his hand.

With frantic hands she searched the vanity behind her for someplace to hide the wand. Her sleek, pocketless dress proved useless in this situation. Her purse lay on the floor by Sam's feet. Only then did she realize the weight of the purse on the handle must have unlocked the door. Damn her carelessness.

While she was distracted, he reached around her and plucked the wand from her fingertips. For a second, awareness flashed through her. He towered over her, larger and taller than he'd ever been before.

She reached for the wand, but was too late. Horror crossed his face as he realized what he held was not a thermometer. He dropped the wand and stepped away, flattening his back against the door as if the pregnancy test wand carried some deadly disease.

Under other circumstances, she might have laughed.

"I told you it wasn't a thermometer."

"Is that a…" He seemed unable to choke out the words.

"Yes. It is." She ran her hands over her face to her temples. She massaged the tender skin, trying to ease the ache pounding through her head.

Sam let out a low whistle. Then he crouched and peered at the wand where it lay on the floor. He didn't touch it.

"There's a plus sign. Positive means good news, right?"

"No, positive means the test is positive. Not that the news is positive." Thirty-two and he didn't know how to read a pregnancy test. Lucky guy.

Almost as if he'd read her thoughts he said, "I've never had to read one of these before."

"How nice for you."

"What are you going to do now?" He stood, wiping his hands on his jeans

"I guess I'm going to ask Bob to marry me."

1

"THAT RAT! That dirty, rotten rat!" Jasmine pounded her delicate fist for emphasis.

Up and down the length of the conference table, heads turned in their direction as Tabitha shushed her friend.

Scooting her chair closer to Jasmine's, she whispered, "Can we just not talk about it?"

"Your boyfriend walks out on you after two years and you don't want to talk about it?"

Of course she didn't want to talk about it. Co-workers surrounded them, the Monday morning meeting would start in less than five minutes, and if Marty, their program director, heard about this, he'd find some way to exploit it. She hadn't meant to tell anyone. But beneath Jasmine's bohemian facade of variable hair color and Celtic tattoos lay the heart of a CIA interrogator.

"I don't want to talk about it *here*," Tabitha tried again.

"You don't want to talk about what?"

She looked up to see Sam standing right behind her. He wore what she teasingly referred to as his uniform: worn jeans, Dingo boots and an untucked, unbuttoned, plaid shirt over a particularly ratty T-shirt. As always, he exuded a scruffy, I-don't-give-a-damn charm that made women melt.

Made other women melt, she mentally corrected.

She spent a lot time shoring up her defenses against men like Sam—the wild, untamable ones. She'd pack her heart in dry ice before she let herself melt over a man like Sam. Not that she was the meltable type. And if she was, she'd melt over a man's accurate day planner and sound five-year plan, not his devil-may-care grin and tousled hair.

Especially not when they belonged to the man who, at the moment, had the power to make her life miserable. Scratch that, more miserable.

He was the only person who knew she was pregnant. Besides Bob, who had scurried to safety when he'd heard the news. It seemed he was a commitment-phobe, as well. Too bad she hadn't recognized it—until now.

What a waste of her time and energy. Bob had seemed like such a safe choice. Two years of stupefying business dinners and coma-inducing dates only to find out steady and responsible weren't the same things after all.

If she'd wanted to end up pregnant and alone she could have accomplished that dating someone considerably more fun than Bob. Someone wild and sexy. Someone like...Sam.

Not Sam, of course—she'd never date anyone at work—but someone like him. It was a moot point, because instead of knee-weakening and irresponsible, she'd unknowingly chosen boring and irresponsible. Either way, she figured too many irresponsible men knew about her pregnancy.

"Nothing," she insisted. She tried to kick Jasmine's leg but missed and stubbed her toe on the table pedestal.

"Bob dumped Tabitha," Jasmine announced just as Sam slid into the chair on Tabitha's other side.

"He did what?" Sam's roar silenced all other conversation and had heads turning in their direction.

Before he could blurt out anything else, she grabbed his hand and yanked him close enough to whisper, "Tell anyone about what happened Friday and you're a dead man."

He raised his eyebrows in question but said nothing. Unfortunately, most of the eyes around the table were still focused on them. A moment later Marty came in.

He paused just inside the door, obviously surprised by the dead silence. Marty always dressed impeccably. Today his slate suit accented the gray at his temples in a way he had to have planned. He looked like the consummate businessman. Which he was. For him, the bottom line was God.

"What's up?" Marty looked around the room. The half dozen other people shrugged. Jasmine, however, shifted in her chair and flipped through her notepad, pretending she hadn't heard.

"Jasmine," Marty called.

"Yes?" She looked up innocently.

"What's up?"

She struggled for an answer, but ultimately caved. "Tabitha's boyfriend dumped her."

Tabitha sucked in her breath. Here it comes. Some scheme or ploy to turn her personal tragedy into a marketing bonanza.

To her surprise, instead of pouncing, Marty looked first at her, then at Sam, assessing them both. Finally, he pinned her with a stare. "So," he barked, "you're single again."

"So it would seem."

"Interesting." Marty lingered over the word.

No one in the room so much as murmured while they watched him with rapt attention.

Sam's expression darkened and Tabitha found herself wondering if he would honor her "request" for silence. She didn't put a whole lot of faith in his discretion.

He gave her a hard time about everything. He'd made jokes on the air the time she'd rushed out of the bathroom with her skirt hem caught in her panty hose. Teased her mercilessly the time she'd interviewed the mayor with her shirt unbuttoned. It was all part of their on-air relationship. He was the joker to her straight man. The Laurel to her Hardy. The yang to her yin.

Which was all well and good on the radio, but she wasn't comfortable trusting Wild Man Sam with the personal knowledge that she was doomed to my-boyfriend's-an-irresponsible-jerk single motherhood.

Glancing in his direction, she saw not the teasing gleam she'd expected but a frown. An all-out scowl really.

Before she could ponder his uncharacteristic expression, Marty reclaimed her attention.

"Tabby, my girl, the listeners love you."

She sat up a little straighter. "Thank you." *I think.*

"They sympathize with you. Men and women alike. You're the darling of the morning airwaves."

Uh-oh.

"And you've just been brutally dumped. The man you loved, the man you trusted, has crushed your fragile heart."

This...

"You're wounded. You're hurt."

...did not...

"Your ego lies in ruins."

...sound good.

"It's perfect!"

"I don't know that I would use the word 'ruins,'" she protested. Marty pegged her with a demanding look. "Sir."

She'd tacked on the "sir" in the hope of placating him. It didn't work.

"Tomorrow morning you will."

"I will?" Did he really expect her to go on the air and talk about being dumped by her boyfriend?

Of course, he did. She was his pet deejay. She always followed through on his ideas and he'd rarely been wrong. But this?

"This tragedy is what the morning show needs. Listeners will tune in every day to hear the ongoing saga of your broken heart. To hear your—" he paused dramatically, hands outstretched "—love letters."

"But, sir, I don't get any love letters." She could only hope Sam wouldn't mention Ted, the divorcee, who e-mailed her with alarming regularity.

"But you will! Starting tomorrow you'll be buried in them." His tone reached the levels of a revival preacher. "You're wounded and heartbroken. The listeners will rally around you, lending you support, helping you rebuild your shattered dignity. They're there for you in your time of need. And soon a new Tabitha will rise like a phoenix from the ashes of personal tragedy. And you'll owe it all to the listeners' love letters."

"Why would they send me letters?" She was afraid she already knew.

"Because each day you'll read through the letters and pick the best one. You'll read the lucky man's letter on the air."

The promotions director nodded along enthusiastically as if jamming to her favorite band. "I like it. It's new. Fun." She paused, cocking her head to the side. "But, Marty, what will they win?"

"Hmm. What will they win?" Marty paused, squinting his eyes and thoughtfully stroking his chin. "The daily winners will each receive a T-shirt, of course. A special, limited-edition, Tabitha T-shirt." He shot a look at the program director. "How soon can we get those?"

She jotted down a few notes, then looked up. "I can have a design for your approval by the end of the day. T-shirts by the end of the week."

T-shirts? They were making T-shirts?

Tabitha sank lower in her chair, trying to catch up with her stomach, which felt as if it had slipped out of her body and lay flopping around on the floor.

"Excellent! The daily winners will get T-shirts. Weekly winners will get a special Love Letters To Tabitha prize pack."

Oh, dear Lord, will the humiliation never end? Tabitha felt her throat tighten and swallowed to loosen the knot forming there.

She glanced around the table. Everyone was watching her, trying to gauge her reaction. The promotions director smiled as she warmed to the idea. Jasmine's face was flushed with guilt. Then there was Sam. He was tapping out an angry rhythm with his pencil.

He fooled a lot of people with his good-natured appearance. His cinnamon-colored hair and laughing gray eyes combined with his bulky six foot frame gave people the impression he was a bear of a man. A teddy bear—cuddly and playful. But she knew better. His cuddly exterior cloaked a will of iron.

Sam watched her. "Aren't you going to say anything?"

She looked up and met Marty's gaze.

"Well, Tabby? What do you think?"

She sucked in a deep breath, nudged Sam's knee under the table as a preventive measure, and smiled brightly. "Sounds really...interesting." Marty narrowed his eyes, assessing her. "Um, so how long will this—" carnival of humiliation "—contest last?"

"Three weeks. There'll be a grand-prize winner. You'll get to pick the lucky man, of course."

The pencil Sam had been tapping against the table snapped in his fingers. The anger written so clearly on his face made her stomach tighten.

She tried to catch his eye, but he was glaring too intently at Marty to notice. So she nudged him with her knee again. This time he nudged back. His gaze met hers across the small table. *Please don't do anything stupid*, she tried to tell him with her eyes.

His gaze darkened with barely suppressed emotion— anger in her defense. She shivered in response. She'd always fought her own battles. And she would fight this one, as well, despite the temptation to let him fight it for her.

Awareness snaked through her. She jerked her knee away from his. Turning her attention back to Marty, she asked, "And the lucky man will win a vacation or something, right?"

"No, no, no. Something much better." His lips curled in a self-satisfied smile. "He'll win a date with you."

In an instant Sam was on his feet. "She's not doing it."

Marty's eyes gleamed with satisfaction. "That's for Tabitha to decide."

Sam leaned forward, planting his palms on the laminated conference table. "She's not doing it, because I'm not doing it."

"You'll both do it if I tell you to."

"There's no way in hell that Tabitha's going to participate in this stupid stunt of yours and there's not a damn thing you can do about it."

Marty didn't even bat an eye. "I can think of several

things, especially with your contract up for review next month."

Before either of them could say another word, Tabitha leaped to her feet. "No! Stop it. Both of you just stop it!" she shrieked.

Every head in the room swiveled in her direction. Eyes widened and mouths gaped. No one looked more shocked by her outburst than Sam. She couldn't have surprised him more if she yelled, "Stop or I'll shoot!"

In fact, the only person more surprised by her outburst was herself. What had come over her? One minute Sam and Marty had been arguing. The next she'd felt five again, huddled in the corner while her parents fought in the next room.

Now that she had everyone's attention, she wasn't quite sure what to do with it. As the expressions turned from shocked to expectant, she shifted nervously.

"I'll..." She took in a shuddering breath. "I'll read the letters. I'll pick the winners. I'll even go on the damn date."

Marty's face split into a smile.

She narrowed her eyes, patently refusing to so much as glance at Sam. "One date. In a very public place. And that's it."

"DAMN IT, TABITHA. Tell him!" Sam demanded from the open door of the building's main entrance. His voice carried across the parking lot, so he stepped outside, following her down the front steps. The noon heat rolled off the asphalt in waves, prickling his skin as it washed over him.

She spun around, forcing him to stop short to keep from bumping into her. "Would you *please* keep it down?" she said in a whispered hiss. Her eyes narrowed.

"I will not tell him. And neither will you. Just stay out of this."

She turned her back to him and stomped toward her car.

For a second he watched her walk away. Damn, she was pissed—at him, as well as the ex-boyfriend, it seemed. Sometimes, he just didn't get women.

What the hell had he done? He was just trying to help. Trying to defend her when she was too good-natured to defend herself.

He jogged a few steps and caught up with her next to her car. She had her knee propped against the car door, her giant bag balanced there.

"Where are they?" she muttered, ignoring him completely. "I just want to go home."

"Tabitha, if you tell him, he won't make you do this."

"Do what?" she demanded without looking up.

"This ridiculous love letter thing. It's just a marketing stunt. It's beneath you."

Now she looked up. But the withering glare she shot him made him wish she hadn't. "This from the man who judged a female mud-wrestling contest last night at Boobies Bar and Grill."

"Barbie's Bar and Grill."

"Right. And I'm sure all those bikini-clad women were just there for the rejuvenative qualities of the mud."

"Hey, men like women who aren't afraid to get a little dirty." He eyed her speculatively. Her royal-blue pantsuit—professional but still feminine—complemented her eyes. He couldn't resist adding, "You should try it sometime."

"What? The mud wrestling or the judging of stupid contests?"

"Getting a little dirty."

"Right. Because the world needs more naked pregnant women covered in mud."

Tabitha mud wrestling? No, he didn't want that. Tabitha naked and ready to get a little dirty? That was something else entirely. A temptation he was smart enough to steer clear of.

He changed tactics. "Okay, don't tell Marty. But you don't have to do this."

"What was I going to do, let him fire you?"

"He wasn't going to fire me."

"Someday you'll push too hard and he will. Today sounded like it could have been that day." She returned her attention to her bag, only to huff in frustration seconds later. "I'm never going to find them."

She walked around to the front of the car and upended the bag onto the hood. Stuff poured out. Ziploc bags filled with granola bars and Hershey's Kisses fell out. Little tubes rolled down and dropped to the ground. Receipts fluttered through the air.

"Aha!" She snagged the keys and started shoving stuff back into the bag.

He grabbed the bag of chocolate kisses. "Isn't chocolate bad for the baby?"

She shot him a withering look. "Like you know."

"I've got a sister with two kids. For eighteen months I listened to her complain about giving up wine, coffee and chocolate."

Doubt flitted across her features. Then she frowned, snatching the chocolate from him. With one brusque motion, she swept the rest of her belongings back into the bag. "Then go bully her." She punctuated the order with a beep from her remote-control key chain as if she could silence him with the gadget.

Before she could climb into her car, he rounded the hood and placed a hand on the doorframe.

She turned around. "Sam, let me go."

Not for the first time he noticed how frail she looked; like the delicate china doll his mother kept propped against a pillow in her guest bedroom. She had the same shoulder-length black hair, the same vivid blue eyes and tiny up-turned nose. Only Tabitha's mouth, full and lush, differed from her porcelain counterpart.

As a child that china doll had been the bane of his existence. A priceless antique and a family heirloom, it had represented everything he hadn't understood about the world of women: beautiful, mysterious, and forever beyond his reach. A toy he hadn't been allowed to play with.

Like that doll, Tabitha tempted him and terrified him. Sometimes it was all he could do to keep his hands off of her. The temptation to...play with her, to get her a little dirty, almost overwhelmed him.

It was a temptation he would not give in to.

She was far more precious to him than any family heirloom. Besides, she held his career in her delicate little hands. Taking her down off her shelf and playing with her might be a hell of a lot of fun, but he wasn't ready to face the consequences.

Almost unwillingly, he brought his other hand to her face, brushing a single curl from her cheek and tucking it behind her ear. He was close enough to see her pupils dilate, enhancing the brilliant blue of her irises. Close enough to hear her sharp intake of breath and to feel her shuddered exhalation against his skin.

He fought his body's response to her nearness, but the success was minor and it left him with too many unanswered questions. Would the rest of her skin feel as silky as the skin of her cheek? What would she do if he pulled her into his arms?

You wanna know what she'd do? She'd knee you in the groin, that's what.

He clenched his fist and dropped his arm, saying, "We're not done here."

"We are."

The steely insistence in her voice snapped him back to reality. She wasn't made of china, she wasn't frail, and she sure as hell wasn't interested in being held in his arms. Tough-as-Nails Tabitha was what one of the guys at the studio called her. And he was right. Tabitha was tough, competent and in control. Always. The only time he'd seen her differently, she'd been sick, puking her guts out and too weak to move. Even then, she'd tried her best to order him around.

Just as she was doing now.

"I'm going home to take a nap. I don't care where you go so long as you mind your own business."

"Marty's going to cash in on your misery and you're willing to let him. If you would just tell him—"

"I'm not ready to tell him yet. I'm not ready to tell any-one."

"Why not? It's not 1950. Being a single mom isn't that big a deal. Fifty percent of the households in America are single-parent families."

"Really?" She eyed him hopefully, then with doubt. "You made that number up, didn't you?"

"Yeah. But it's still a lot."

"I know." She sighed and the sound was full of a life-time of regret. "But it wasn't going to be me. I had my life all planned out. I was going to do everything right. I guess this is what I get for planning too far ahead."

"Are you thinking of not keeping the baby?"

For a moment she didn't meet his gaze. But when she did, there were no doubts, no waverings. "I'm going to keep it. I just need more time to figure out how to handle things."

"This isn't something you can hide forever."

"Well, duh. You think I don't know that? In about four months, I'll balloon up like the Goodyear blimp, but until then this is my secret. Besides, I haven't even been to the doctor yet. Those store-bought tests aren't a hundred-percent accurate."

"For Pete's sake, Tabitha. You only did one?"

"No. I did more than that, but it's possible they could all be wrong."

"How many did you do?"

She frowned and looked away. "Twelve."

"Damn, Tabitha, twelve pregnancy tests and you still have doubts? Snap out of it, honey. You're in denial."

Her eyes shot to his. "Don't 'honey' me. We're not on the radio and I don't have to put up with your macho shtick for the listeners' amusement."

He didn't budge. "Tell me this much... When that bastard dumped you, was it before or after you told him about the baby?"

She flushed a furious red. "After. It was after I told him."

When he muttered a curse, her eyes narrowed and she asked, "What? Doesn't that please you? Another man has escaped the noose of matrimony, right? I'm surprised you aren't dancing in the streets."

"Damn it, that's not what I'm thinking and you know it."

"Really? Well, that's a first coming from you, the staunchest supporter of single men. Because marriage is an institution and who wants to live in an institution, right? Isn't that what you always say?"

Her voice rose sharply and he couldn't tell if she was angry or on the verge of tears. Either way, he didn't know what to do about it. This wasn't the Tabitha he knew. His Tabitha was calm and in control. Certainly not this snarling virago.

She shoved at his shoulder, making his hand slip from its position on the top of her car. "Well, guess what, buddy? Bob is different. He's not like you and the other Peter Pan wannabes. He's responsible."

"Yeah, he's a real stand-up guy." He didn't bother to hide his contempt. As far as he was concerned, Bob wasn't—and never had been—worthy of Tabitha.

She bristled. "Sure he's scared. Who wouldn't be? I'm scared! But he's going to come to his senses. And when he does, he'll remember that he loves me. And he *will* ask me to marry him. You can bet on that."

"Damn it, I didn't mean—"

But before he could explain, she opened her door, climbed into her car and slammed the door.

"Tabitha, wait!" Frustrated, he slapped his hand on the hood of her car as she shifted into gear then pulled out of the parking space.

He watched as the dark blue sedan disappeared down the hill. Damn it!

Why couldn't he have just kept his mouth shut? If she wanted to throw herself at an asshole like Bob, it wasn't any of his business.

He cursed himself for wishing it was.

Over the past two years he'd spent a lot of time maintaining his defenses against Tabitha. They worked together every day. And the show required a closeness—a give-and-take—that he didn't have with any other woman. But outside of the studio, they both maintained their distance, emotionally and physically.

Their relationship worked because they kept it carefully contained. Squeezed into the confines of their on-air time.

Today that emotional energy had begun to seep out. But he wasn't about to the let it spill over into the rest of his life.

His resolve hardened, he turned to head back inside, but stopped short when he saw Marty standing not ten feet away, grinning in anticipation.

"So what's got our little Tabby in such a snit?" Marty asked.

"Couldn't you tell?" he countered, carefully watching Marty, trying to figure out how much the manipulative bastard had heard.

"Enough to know there'll be tension on the air tomorrow." Marty smiled broadly, rubbing his hands together. "A little lovers' spat on the air is always good for ratings."

"Just what the hell is that supposed to mean?" Normally he'd just let it go, but today...after taking so much crap from Tabitha... Today, he wasn't in the mood. "You know damn well there's nothing between us."

"That's where you're wrong, my boy. There's chemistry. You know it. I know it. And most importantly, the listeners know it. Chemistry makes you a great pair, makes our morning show the best in town."

"You're full of crap, old man."

Yes, they did have chemistry, on and off the air. But Marty was wrong if he thought that meant they were primed to get involved romantically. Tabitha wasn't interested in him—she'd made that clear plenty of times. Besides, she was still holding out for Bob.

Without responding to Marty's taunts, Sam turned and made to walk back into the building. Marty stopped him on the steps with a hand on his arm.

"You say what's on your mind, Sam. That's what I like about you—"

"I didn't think there was anything you liked about me."

Marty smiled that snake-oil-salesman smile of his. "That's what I like about you," he repeated. "But watch yourself on the air. You give in too soon and the audience will lose interest."

Then the bastard winked, turned and sauntered down the steps, whistling. And it took everything in Sam's power not to push him down the rest of the stairs.

2

"OH, NO. What are you two doing here?" Tabitha eyed Jasmine and Chandi with trepidation. Who knew a best friend and beloved sister could stir up such anxiety?

"We come bearing gifts," Chandi announced, elbowing her way past Tabitha and holding up a canvas Whole Foods grocery bag as proof. "Solace, comfort foods, and female bonding."

"And wine," Jasmine added, also entering uninvited.

Tabitha glared at Jasmine. "You told."

"Of course I told. What was I supposed to do? Tomorrow morning you're announcing the contest and the whole city will know."

"Besides—" Chandi set her bag on the kitchen table and began unloading it "—how can I be a supportive younger sister when you don't tell me what's going on in your life?"

"You really should have told her yourself," Jasmine chided.

Dear God, why had she ever introduced them?

Holding up her hands in a gesture of innocence, she protested, "I was going to call. But I knew your finals were coming up and I didn't want to distract you."

Chandi pulled out the last of the take-out boxes and propped her hands on her hips. "Finals? You think I'd let finals get in the way of comforting you in your time of need? What kind of sister do you take me for?"

"Actually, no, I didn't think you'd let finals get in your way. That's why I didn't call."

Chandi set aside the empty bag. "You know what your problem is, Tabitha?"

"No, but I'm pretty sure you're going to tell me."

"You're too self-contained. You try so hard to be independent. You've always got to be the strong one. You nurture everyone else, but you never let anyone nurture you."

"But...I..."

"She's right." Jasmine nodded.

"But..."

"You need to let us take care of you." Jasmine set down the bottle of wine and headed for the kitchen. She returned a few seconds later with three glasses and a corkscrew. "We got white. Is that okay?"

Tabitha eyed the bottle with longing. There were moments in life—such as this one, trapped between a pushy sister and a nosy best friend—when wine seemed like the perfect solution.

She sighed. "I'll stick with water."

Chandi and Jasmine turned simultaneously to stare in shock. "Water?"

Tabitha forced a smile. "I've been...feeling really dehydrated today. The heat, you know."

Chandi frowned, but Jasmine merely shrugged. To escape from her sister's scrutiny, she retrieved plates from the kitchen and began distributing the take-out. Even without the wine, she took comfort in the familiarity of the act. She didn't need to ask who got what. Chandi was always the vegan eggplant Parmesan, Jasmine always the chicken tacos, she the turkey sandwich. Twice a month for nearly two years, the three of them had been buying take-out from the Whole Foods deli for girls' night out.

She stilled, a serving spoon hovering over Chandi's eggplant. How would the baby change things? Chandi and Jasmine would never abandon her, but girls' night out would be different. From now on, everything would be different.

"Don't you dare cry!" Jasmine's words brought Tabitha out of her reverie. Jasmine thumped her palm on the table, rattling her wineglass. "He's just not worth it!"

"What?" Tabitha looked up and blinked. Only then did she realize she was blinking away tears.

"Bob isn't worth it. He's not worth your time and he's not worth your tears."

"I wasn't crying over him." She lowered herself to her chair, surprised by the truth of her words. His desertion made her angry—frustrated her—but it hadn't broken her heart.

She didn't love Bob. She'd wanted to, tried to, but never had. Maybe in her heart she'd always known what her brain hadn't been ready to accept. Bob just wasn't right for her.

With a sigh, she met Chandi's gaze. "I just wish..."

She didn't let herself finish the thought.

"Don't worry," Chandi said fiercely. "You'll find someone else. Someone much better."

Someone else? Some other man in which she'd have to invest time and energy only to be told after two years that he wasn't sure? No thanks. Besides, what man was going to take on an instant family?

"I don't think so."

But Jasmine misinterpreted her answer. "Bob isn't the only man out there."

"I know that. I'll be fine."

"Great," Chandi said. "Then you're ready."

"Ready for what?"

"A blind date." Chandi stabbed a bite of eggplant. She looked at Jasmine. "I was thinking of my Japanese Medieval History professor."

"The really cute one with the British accent?"

"But..."

"Yep, that's the one."

"Sounds perfect. We'll schedule him for next week."

"But..."

"I was thinking—"

Tabitha stood, bumping her chair back with her legs, and propped her fists on her hips. "No! No blind dates."

Jasmine and Chandi blinked in surprise. Jasmine dropped her fork and narrowed her eyes. "But you're going on a date with whoever wins the contest."

"Well, yes. But I don't seem to have much of a choice."

"So you trust the station to set you up." Chandi frowned, her sea-green eyes rounding into the sad-puppy expression that had always kicked Tabitha in the gut. "But you don't trust us?"

"It's not like that." Neither Jasmine nor Chandi seemed to notice her insistence. "It's just one date. A publicity thing."

"My professor is so cute," Chandi explained to Jasmine.

"I know." Jasmine patted Chandi's hand.

"He's handsome and sophisticated. He's got that sexy intellectual thing going on."

"If he's so great, why does he need his students setting him up on blind dates?" Tabitha asked.

"He's perfect. Smart. Funny. Kind of anal, like you."

"I'm not anal."

Jasmine shot her a look of withering disdain. "Oh puh-lease. You're so anal you could date a proctologist."

"I'm not anal. I'm structured."

"There's a difference?"

"Okay, so I'm not like either of you. I can't just float through life."

"I know," Chandi said. "You always needed to be the responsible one."

"Someone had to be." A tiny flash of resentment flared within her, but she doused it. "I just...I need that structure. I need to know I've got good health insurance and that I'm putting enough of my salary into a retirement fund. I need that security."

Jasmine and Chandi both nodded, as if they understood completely. Then Chandi ruined the effect by asking, "Why can't you have security and a blind date?"

Sometimes it was like trying to explain upper-level physics to a child.

Shaking her head, she said, "It's just too soon."

"Too soon?" Chandi eyed Tabitha. "You said you weren't crying over him."

"I..." Tabitha shifted under the intensity of her sister's gaze. Exhaustion, which had been creeping up on her all day, now ambushed her. She sat back in her chair, her throat convulsing over the bite she'd just taken. Struggling to swallow, she blinked. "It was just sudden."

Chandi reached across the table and grabbed Tabitha's hand. "It wasn't sudden. He was never right for you."

"But—"

"There's no but about it," Jasmine insisted. "Bob was all wrong for you."

"Abso-freaking-lutely!"

"Hold on." Tabitha held up a hand to stop the flow of conversation. "What do you mean, all wrong for me?"

Jasmine and Chandi looked at each other and then shrugged as if silently agreeing to something.

"He was just...all wrong for you," Chandi admitted.

"You mean to tell me I was dating someone for a year and a half and you both thought he was all wrong for me."

They nodded.

"Yeah."

"Pretty much."

"Why didn't either of you say something?"

"We thought you knew."

"If I knew, why would I continue dating him?"

"We thought he was just temporary," Jasmine said.

"Yeah. It's not like we would have let you marry him and bear his children or anything."

What perfect timing. "Bob wasn't that bad," she said weakly.

Jasmine and Chandi looked at each other, then started to laugh.

"What?"

"You're right," Jasmine said. "Alone, he wasn't. But the two of you together were like that couple from the American Gothic painting."

Chandi, after making a serious effort to control her laughter, said, "Do you remember what you said about him after you came home from your first date?"

"No."

"You said, 'Finally someone who takes financial planning seriously.'"

Jasmine erupted into peals of laughter.

Tabitha narrowed her gaze and shot them both a "drop dead" look. "So now I'm just some boring American Gothic person?"

Instantly, Jasmine and Chandi stopped laughing.

Jasmine grabbed her hand. "No, hon, you're not. You're wonderful. We love that you're responsible and upstanding and all that other stuff."

"Yeah. I know better than anyone why you're anal and structured and grounded. You spent your whole childhood needing to be that way. You were the only one with any parenting skills. But I'm grown up now and Mom has William to take care of her. You don't need to be a parent anymore. You can cut loose a little now. You don't need to be with a man who's even more grounded than you."

Don't I? What she needed was someone who could change diapers, heat milk... Yeah, men like that were all over the place.

"Right," Jasmine agreed. "A relationship needs balance. You need someone who brings out your playful side, makes you laugh. Someone who gets your juices going."

"Oh, yeah," Chandi said. "Someone who can mix things up a little."

Tabitha sighed. "You're describing a kitchen appliance, not a man."

"That's not a bad analogy," Chandi said. "You want a man who's powerful and well built."

"Guaranteed to last a lifetime," Jasmine added. "And when you turn him on, he knows how to stir things up."

"Like a really nice blender?" Tabitha asked.

"Exactly!" Jasmine said. "Equally good for late-night margaritas and early morning smoothies."

What about late-night feedings and mushed bananas?

"That was Bob's problem," Chandi said. "He was more like a toaster oven. Serviceable, but you don't want to spend your life cooking with one."

Tabitha poked restlessly at her half-eaten sandwich.

Maybe they were right. Maybe Bob had reinforced all of her most boring qualities. Maybe she should rethink her strategy. These next few months might be her only opportunity to have any fun for a very long time.

She looked up at Chandi. "So you think this history professor is my blender?"

Chandi frowned. "Maybe more of a mini food processor."

"Which is just fine, hon. 'Cause after a couple of years of Mr. Toaster Oven, you're gonna have to work your way up to blender."

Long after Chandi and Jasmine had finished the wine, cleaned off the table and headed home, Tabitha lay in bed contemplating kitchen appliances. She'd known and dated a lot of toaster ovens in her life.

Chandi teased her about being attracted to the most boring men, but Chandi didn't know the truth. In reality, she wasn't attracted to the toaster ovens at all. She was attracted to the wild ones, the untamable men. The men like Sam.

She was attracted to them...but a little scared of them, as well. The wild ones were a little too out of control, and though that turned her on, it wasn't what she needed.

She needed a stable guy. Someone steady. The kind of guy she'd thought Bob was. So for all these years, she'd been carefully sublimating her desire for what she really wanted and giving herself what she thought she needed. It was like craving tiramisu and eating brussel sprouts instead. Or, to keep the metaphor going, craving a mocha malt but only letting yourself have whole-wheat toast.

Still, Chandi and Jasmine were right. None of the toaster ovens were built to last a lifetime and certainly none of them made her juices flow.

If she was honest with herself, she already knew one

very well-built blender. Sam. The only man who'd ever stirred her up inside.

But Sam wouldn't last a lifetime. He was the kind of blender a girl would be lucky to get a couple months use out of. And she couldn't have Sam anyway. She didn't care how good he would look in her kitchen.

Her whole career was based on how well she and Sam got along on the air. From day one, they'd clicked. Sometimes she wondered if they would click off the air, as well. But that was something she would never find out.

Sure, she had the occasional waking dream about what it would be like to be with Sam. It'd be great. At first. Sam was funny, sexy...wild enough to make a girl wonder. But it wouldn't last. Sam's relationships never did.

She'd seen the pattern over and over again in the deluge of women flooding Sam's life. She used to tease him mercilessly about it. Then the river of women thinned to a stream, which then slowed to a trickle.

She could only assume the women were still out there and he just wasn't bringing them by the station anymore. Women certainly still threw themselves at him. Flirting with him when they called the station and passing him their numbers at remotes. Even if he dated only a fraction of them, the numbers were still absurd.

Stop thinking about it! she chastised herself. *It's not your business. It never was and it never will be.*

Sam—blender that he was—would crush her heart like margarita ice. And she'd have to face him every morning over a microphone. She'd have to be fun, flirty and clever, all while trying to hide her broken heart. It didn't take a genius to figure out how well that would work out.

So where did that leave her?

Wanting the blender, dating the mini food processor, but willing to settle for the toaster oven.

Because if Bob wanted to get back together, she'd have to give him another chance. For the sake of her child.

"AND THAT'S A LOOK at today's traffic," Jasmine chirped. "Now back to you, Sam."

"This is K-O-N-E. Austin's number-one choice for hit music," Sam crooned into the microphone. "Coming your way this hour is the latest installment of Love Letters To Tabitha. Don't forget, tomorrow she'll pick this week's winner." He lingered over the words, his tone insinuating the sizzle to come. "But first, we've got another twenty minutes of great music."

Tabitha stopped listening as he rattled off the list of coming songs. Pulling her earphones off, she massaged her neck.

With a resigned sigh, she reached for a saltine. At least no one at the station had noticed the stash of crackers she'd been carrying around for the past few days. Although she didn't want anyone to notice the crackers, it annoyed her that no one had. Was she invisible?

She shoved another cracker into her mouth to quell the bitter taste of her resentment.

"Do the crackers help?"

She looked up to find Sam watching her, his earphones off and microphone pushed away as a twenty-minute music set played in the background. So someone had noticed, after all.

She nodded and smiled, despite a mouthful of crackers. After choking them down with a swig of weak tea, she said, "A little."

Before she could offer up the apology she'd been mentally preparing for the past week, he asked, "Can't the doctor give you something for the morning sickness?"

She said nothing and didn't meet his eyes, deliberately focusing her attention on the crackers.

"Tell me you've seen the doctor."

"Not yet," she whispered, even though the studio was soundproof.

"Tabitha—" he started angrily.

"My appointment's tomorrow afternoon."

"Good." He nodded wisely, flipping through the pages in front of him, then added casually, "I'll go with you."

Shock rocked her back in her chair. "Why would you do that?"

"You shouldn't go alone."

"I'll be fine. I haven't needed anyone to take me to the doctor since I learned to drive when I was fifteen."

"Liar," he teased without looking up from his papers.

"What?"

"Remember last year when you had the flu?"

"Oh, yeah." How could she have forgotten that? She'd felt too weak to roll to the other side of the bed to answer the phone. Then, what seemed like hours later, Sam had nudged her awake, helped her dress and carried her out to the car. "I forgot."

"Yeah, well, I didn't. Took me four days to clean out the back of the car."

"Thanks for reminding me." Now that she thought about it, she was surprised he hadn't mentioned it before now. Losing her cookies in his back seat seemed precisely the kind of thing he would tease her about.

She was still contemplating the issue when he repeated, "I'll go with you. Someone needs to be there to make sure you follow the doctor's orders. He'll probably have a long list of things you should do and I don't want you ignoring his advice."

"Her."

"What?"

"Her advice. My doctor is a woman. And my appointment's at three-thirty."

"I'll pick you up at three at your place."

She nodded, a smile tugging at the corners of her lips. She'd surprised herself by giving in so easily. It wasn't like her. She didn't like to depend on other people. Too often they let you down, a lesson she'd learned often enough as a child.

Besides, it wasn't Sam's place to go with her. By rights, it was Bob's place. Bob, the deserter. Bob, the loser.

Bob, who didn't want to be with her anymore.

"BECCA, GAIL, time for bed!"

At the sound of his sister's voice, Sam paused, his three-year-old niece, Becca, dangling upside down from his arms. He jostled her and her arms flailed inches above the toy-strewn floor. A riot of giggles erupted.

Gail, his five-year-old niece, launched herself at his legs. "Unca Sam, put her down. Mommy says it's time for bed."

"Put her down?" he asked innocently, swinging her by the legs.

"Yes! Put her down."

"You mean, just let her go right now?"

Gail giggled. "Yes!"

"Well, okay." He raised her high above his head as though to let her drop. She squealed in delight.

"Sam?"

Sam spun around to see his sister standing in the living room doorway, her arms crossed and her shoulder propped against the jamb. He wasn't fooled by her scowl.

"It'll take hours to get them to sleep after this."

He carefully righted Becca and set her on the floor. "I'll read to them."

She stepped into the room. "No. It's a weeknight. They'll talk you into reading dozens of stories and you'll be back there for hours. Not tonight."

"Just two stories. I promise."

"Three, Unca Sam. Can you read three?"

Marie must have seen him wavering. She pried Gail from his legs and picked up Becca. "Honestly, Sam. When you have kids of your own, you can't be such a pushover."

He kissed each of the girls, hugging them until Marie carried them off to brush their teeth. Over her shoulder, Marie muttered, "Wimp," as she steered them toward the bathroom.

While waiting for Marie to return, he nudged aside a pile of plastic fruit with his shoe, navigated around a stack of Lego bricks, and worked his way closer to his sister's bookshelf. Stacks of books competed for space with framed photos of Becca and Gail. An infant Gail dressed as a pumpkin rested on a stack of computer books. Becca holding an Easter basket propped up a half-dozen gardening books. And beneath the picture of the four of them at Disney World was a stash of pregnancy books.

He jerked his hand away as if the books hid a nest of snakes. Then he stepped back to view them from a safer distance, but their cheerful pastel spines held his attention.

He was curious, that was all. No harm in that, right?

Besides, Tabitha was going to need help—whether she wanted to admit it or not. And he'd guess not.

Truth be told, he needed help, too. He had enough trouble keeping his hands off the Tough-as-Nails Tabitha she'd been for the past couple of years. He hoped the china-doll Tabitha who'd been showing up over the past couple of weeks wasn't here to stay, because it'd be damn near impossible to keep his hands off of her.

But he knew Tabitha. Once she'd been to the doctor, once she'd armed herself with a little information, which he would willingly provide, once she was back in control, she'd be tough as nails again.

And he wouldn't have to fight this ridiculous urge to take care of her.

Sam skimmed his finger down the spines. *What to Expect When You're Expecting.* Too serious. *The Girlfriend's Guide to Pregnancy.* Too feminine. *Pregnancy for Dummies.* Jackpot.

He wiggled the book out from the bottom of the stack and began thumbing through it. Twenty minutes later, when his sister stumbled back into the room and flopped down beside him on the sofa, he was staring at a sonogram picture of a fetus.

"Whatcha looking at?"

He rotated the book and squinted. "A baby. Supposedly." He turned the book another ninety degrees.

Marie reached over and took the book from him. She shot him a surprised look, then handed it back right-side up. "You always were the weird one."

Staring at the grainy black-and-white image, he frowned. "Is this like those magic eye pictures where you have to unfocus your gaze?"

"No, doofus, you're just not looking at it right." She pointed to a white splotch near the top of the photo. "That's the head—" she trailed her finger down the page to another splotch "—and there's the body."

"Oh, right." He snapped the book closed, unwilling to admit he still saw nothing but splotches. "Can I borrow this?"

"Sure." Marie pulled her legs up onto the sofa and tucked them under her.

He tossed the book onto the coffee table, then propped his foot on the edge beside it. "Is chocolate bad for pregnant women?"

"Only because it's empty calories. And if you eat a lot of it, the caffeine might be a problem, but in small amounts it's fine." Marie leaned forward, a speculative gleam in her eye. "So what's with the sudden interest in babies?"

"Well...it's because...we're sponsoring the baby expo next month. I need pregnancy trivia. That's why."

"Oh." Marie looked a little confused, but she seemed to buy it. "I heard about Bob and Tabitha. How's she taking it?"

"Hard to say. She doesn't really believe he's gone."

"So what are you going to do about it?"

"About what? I can't make her accept that he's an ass."

"Not that, silly. Now that he's gone, are you finally going to ask her out?"

"What?" He cleared his throat. "I mean, why would I do that?"

"We assumed Bob was the only thing keeping y'all apart."

"'We'? Who's we?"

"Everyone. Everybody who listens to the show. You guys are so great together on the air."

"That's because we're professionals."

"Nonsense. You're a good team. Before she was added to the show, your ratings weren't nearly this good."

"Thanks, sis, for rubbing it in."

"Don't act wounded. You were good on your own. With her, you're great. Now that Bob's gone, why not ask her out?"

"Tabitha and I can't go out. We work together."

"Why not?"

"It'd be awkward. Maybe not at first, but eventually."

"Dave and I work together. It isn't awkward."

"That's because you and Dave got married, bought a house in the suburbs and had a couple of kids. That's not how it would be with Tabitha and me."

"Why not?"

"You know me and women. I've never had a relationship that lasted more than four or five months."

"So?"

"So what would happen with Tabitha? We'd go out a couple of months, half a year tops, then when we broke up, everything would be different. How long do you think she'd be willing to sit by and watch me go out with someone else?"

Or worse, how long would he able to watch her with another man? Watching her with Bob these past two years had been bad enough when he had just his imagination fueling his fantasies. How much harder would it be to watch her with another man once he'd made love to her?

"Soo-oo," Marie said, "don't break up with her."

"It's not that simple."

Marie shrugged, but her expression made it clear she thought he was being an idiot. "Of course it is. You don't break up with her. You live happily ever after. Happens all the time."

Sure, she made it sound simple. But she didn't know what he knew. Even with Bob gone, Tabitha's life had gotten very messy. "Well, it doesn't happen to me. And it's not going to."

"Why not?"

"I'm just not ready to settle down, that's all. Besides, I'm not marriage material."

"Not marriage material? You're kidding, right?" When he shook his head, she scoffed. "You're perfect marriage material. You may fool other people with that Wild Man Sam act you've perfected for the radio. But I know the truth."

"What's that supposed to mean?"

"On the radio, you've created the persona of a carefree bachelor. Wild, reckless, and untamed. And that's fine for the radio, but that's not who you are."

"Okay, genius. Then who am I?"

"Deep down inside, you're as stable and responsible as a Republican president." Her eyes flashed with laughter as she teased him. "You are nothing more than a sheep in wolf's clothing."

He laughed at the image. "You sure about that?"

"Positive." The laughter in her eyes dimmed and she placed a hand on his arm. "I remember what you were like growing up. When Dad died, you took it into your head that you were the man of the family. You took responsibility for Lizzy and me."

He shifted uncomfortably. "Mom was busy at work. Somebody had to take care of you."

"You were only ten. She relied on you too much."

"Until she met Roger, she didn't have anyone else she could rely on."

He'd been nineteen when his mother met and married his stepfather. He'd never felt like Roger was a father to him the way he was to Marie and Lizzy. But after nine years as the man of the family, he'd gratefully handed over his position to Roger.

"I'm just saying that I understand you enjoy being single and carefree," Marie continued. "Fine. You've certainly earned the right. But someday—someday soon—that won't be enough. You'll realize you want to settle down."

"Maybe. But if I was the kind of guy who could make a long-term relationship work, don't you think I'd have had one by now?" He stood, shoving his hands into his pockets.

"Not when you always put your career first."

"I haven't met a woman yet who could make me want to put her before my career."

"I think you have met her. I think you're just too scared to admit it."

He didn't let himself think too much about his sister's words until he was on his way home, driving down MoPac from suburban Roundrock into downtown.

Marie was way off base on this one. He wasn't ready to settle down. Maybe he never would be.

He'd never regretted sacrificing his own childhood for Marie and Lizzy—he'd do it all over again if he had to—but he'd sure been happy to get on with his own life. As soon as his mom and Roger tied the knot, he'd left for college and never looked back.

His life was just the way he wanted it. He was responsible for no one other than himself. Life was simple.

No woman was—or ever would be—more important to him than his career. Certainly not Tabitha.

Sure, he cared about her, but it was impersonal. They were partners, after all. And yes, he was attracted to her. But that was it. Just attraction.

She was a beautiful, intelligent, funny woman and they'd been working closely together for years. He'd have to be a monk not to be attracted to her. A dead monk.

But that didn't mean he was going to screw up his career over her. No way.

3

FIVE WEEKS PREGNANT.

She was not only pregnant; she was five weeks pregnant.

Only thirty-three weeks left of normal life. Subtract from that at least sixteen weeks of blimphood, and life looked pretty grim.

As she left the doctor's office and crossed the street to the pharmacy, she couldn't stop thinking about it. After today, there could be no doubt. No more fooling herself.

Sam was here to make sure of that. He wasn't letting her get away with anything. Even now he stood by her side, silently waiting for the light to change, his hand cupping her elbow. The gesture seemed protective, yet she wondered if he wasn't holding on to her because he suspected she might bolt.

What did he think she was going to do? Break free and make a mad dash for the maternity store?

The light changed and they crossed to the small neighborhood pharmacy. As Sam held open the door for her, she turned to him and said, "You don't have to come with me. I'm perfectly capable of filling my own prescriptions."

"Tough. I'm not letting you out of my sight until they're filled. I'm not going to let you put it off like you did the doctor's appointment or taking the test or telling

Marty. This is too important. For your health and the baby's."

"Oh, so now I'm getting health tips from a man whose idea of a balanced breakfast is beef jerky washed down with a gallon of coffee."

"Meat and caffeine, the two most important food groups." He flashed her a smile. "Besides, the women I make breakfast for never complain."

She rolled her eyes in mock exasperation. Truth was, she'd always felt a little sorry for the nameless, faceless women Sam joked about. Now she wondered if her pity was tinged with jealously. To hide her confusion she said, "I suppose you're going to tell me they're too satisfied to complain about breakfast."

"Hey, you said it, not me."

"Frankly, Sam, I'm surprised you let any of them stay for breakfast." She tilted her head and studied him. "Unless that's why you eat jerky and coffee for breakfast. Because it's fast. If you cooked, a woman she might interpret that as a sign you were ready to settle down."

"Well, Tabby, if you're a bacon fan, just let me know. I can always pick some up at the store."

Even though she knew he was kidding, her body still pulsed in response to his suggestive comment.

Before she could respond, however, they reached the pharmacist's counter. The college-aged young man standing behind it asked, "Can I help you?"

She temporarily shelved her commentary on the dining habits of the North American bachelor. Instead she handed over the prescriptions and her insurance card to the boy.

He glanced down at the card. "Hmm, Tabitha Talbot. That sounds familiar." He looked up, head cocked to the side. "Hey, you're not the Tabitha from the radio, are you?"

Tabitha eyed the boy speculatively. Blue hair, multiple piercings. Probably a fan of alt-rock or maybe even industrial grunge. Hardly K-O-N-E's target audience. Nevertheless, she smiled at him and nodded.

"Wow!" he gushed. "This is so cool. I love your show. I listen every day on the way to work." He leaned across the counter. "This contest rocks! Do you want to hear my letter?"

The boy dropped the card and the prescription to pat his pockets. Before he could pull out a letter, Tabitha reached out, grabbed the insurance card and the prescription, and backed up into Sam's chest.

"I can't get this filled here," she whispered over her shoulder. "He'll know." She looked pointedly in the boy's direction.

"Then you shouldn't have told him who you were," he whispered back.

"Look at him," she whispered. "He's not in our demographic. I figured he knew my name only because his mom listened." Then, in an overly loud voice, she said, "You know, on second thought, I don't need to have this filled today." She waved the slip of paper in the air, edging around Sam. "I'll wait and do it later." She cleared her throat, still backing up toward the door. "I, um, look forward to getting that letter. Can't stay to chat about it, though. Contest rules, you know."

With that, she spun and dashed for the door, nearly knocking over a metal book rack on her way out. Sam exhaled slowly and reluctantly met the boy's eyes. He looked to Sam for explanation.

He shrugged. "It's the breakup."

"Oh," the kid replied, his brow furrowing with concern.

"It's been hard on her." The kid nodded in sympathetic understanding. "Stressful. She's very...vulnerable. But don't worry. She'll be back to her old self soon. Very soon."

The kid gestured to the folded paper in his hand. "I better keep working on this letter. She needs all the help she can get."

We all do, kid. We all do.

THREE STORES LATER, Tabitha was sure Sam was wishing he'd never offered to come with her. But now he was stuck with her. Well, not *with* her, exactly.

Ten minutes ago he'd settled her onto the waiting bench in the pharmacy/grocery, shoved a copy of *American Parenting Magazine* into her hands, and dashed off to pick up some food while she waited. She stared at the magazine for a second before tossing it aside in disgust.

Feeling antsy, she sprawled out on the bench and resigned herself to people watching.

Grocery stores in the middle of day were not, as a rule, great receptacles of fascinating people. She seemed to see the same person over and over. Mothers. Young mothers, carting around one or two rosy-cheeked cherubs. The late-in-life mothers, talking to their children as if they were the board members of the company the woman had left behind. The type-A mothers, rushing through the store, dressed in workout clothes, pushing carts full of fresh veggies. The mothers of teenage boys, pushing one cart and pulling another, both of them overflowing with calorie-laden food.

As she watched, a different woman broke through the parade of mothers. A tall, slender blonde, not pushing a cart, but carrying a bottle of wine in one hand, a bundle of flowers in the other and a loaf of French bread under her arm. This woman had a life. The life Tabitha was saying goodbye to in thirty-three weeks.

She watched the woman stop to scan a display of cards.

"Ma'am," called a nasal voice from behind her. "Ma'am, your prescription's ready."

Only then did she realized the "ma'am" had been directed at her. When had she become a ma'am?

Numbly, she rose from the bench to accept the white pharmacy bag from the young man. She fumbled with the ten-dollar co-pay, trying to keep her expression blank, not wanting this kid to know he'd skewered her already floundering self-confidence.

She turned around, intending to head straight for the door, and was surprised to find Sam standing right behind her. He'd already been through the checkout line and now held several grocery sacks. Wordlessly, she allowed him to lead her from the store.

She could only imagine the kind of food Sam would buy for a pregnant woman, but right now she felt too emotionally exhausted to face shopping on her own. Besides, he'd been helpful today. She didn't want to hurt his feelings by pointing out the nutritional failings of any food bearing the words "Cup o'."

"Look, this really isn't necessary," she insisted twenty minutes later as he carried her grocery bags through the living room of her small fifties-style ranch house. She hung her purse on the hat rack by the door and her keys on the tiny hook beside it.

She smiled brightly and held out her hands. "If you'll just hand over those groceries, you can be on your way."

He ignored her. "Kitchen's back here?" He didn't wait

for her answer but headed through the living room toward the arched doorway leading to the kitchen.

"Just set the bags on the counter," she called as she slipped off her shoes and nudged them under a bench by the door. As always, tension seeped from her the second her bare feet touched the oak floorboards. Odd how even the soles of her feet knew what home felt like.

For a moment she waited, barefoot and hopeful, to see if he would do as she asked. When she heard a string of muttered curses from the kitchen, she knew he'd made the mistake of trying to put away her groceries.

Shoulders sloped with resignation, she followed the curses like breadcrumbs. He glanced up when she walked into the room. She felt a tinge of rebellion. What right did he have to rummage through her cabinets?

"Where's your food?" he asked over his shoulder before turning his attention back to the task of opening then slamming shut each of her empty cabinets.

Annoyed by his presumption, she crossed to his side, slapping a cabinet door so that it snapped closed a nanosecond after he jerked his fingers away.

"Not that it's any of your business, but my food is there." She nodded in the direction of the refrigerator. As far as she was concerned, her fridge held all the food she needed on hand: a bag of bagels and two kinds of cream cheese, low fat for every day and whipped raspberry for special occasions. The bagels were her sole concession to the culinary arts.

"You should have said something. I would have bought—"

She didn't let him finish. "I don't need anything else. I don't cook."

"What do you mean, you don't cook? Everybody cooks."

"I didn't say I couldn't cook. I said I don't. I choose not to. I eat out. Or I get take-out. I wouldn't even keep the bagels, but there's no place open at five-thirty in the morning."

"You eat out?" He spoke slowly, shaking his head, as if still trying to grasp the concept. "I know you eat out at lunch, but dinner, too?"

"Yes. Dinner, too. Lots of people do it."

After cooking dinner every night from the time she was eight to the time she was eighteen, she hated to cook. And when she'd moved out of her mother's house and into the dorm, she'd sworn she would never again lift another saucepan, touch another spatula, or tear open another packet of orange-powdered cheese. And she hadn't.

"Well, you should start cooking. Whatever you're eating out can't be good for the baby."

Stubbornly she said, "It's kept me going all this time."

"That's not good enough anymore."

"And I'm supposed to take advice from you? I've seen the way you eat."

"Not the beef jerky again."

"Well, yeah. Exactly."

"Beef jerky is a nearly fat-free source of protein, which is exactly what you need in the morning for energy."

"Right, and I'm sure that's why you eat it, because you're such a nutrition expert."

His eyes narrowed in irritation. "I'm going to ignore your sarcasm, 'cause you've had a long day." He leaned his hip against her counter, taking up far more of the kitchen than she thought necessary, as he ticked off her nutritional deficiencies on his fingers. "I know enough about nutrition to know you're probably not eating enough vegetables. You're definitely not getting enough calcium. I checked—there's no calcium in creamer. But don't worry, I bought you lots of stuff."

As he turned his back on her to dig through the bag, she stuck out her tongue. However, any satisfaction she got from her silent rebellion was quickly enveloped by her anxiety as she saw what Sam was pulling from the sack. Veggies. Milk. Chocolate milk. Strawberry milk. They still made strawberry milk?

And yogurt. He pulled out container after container of yogurt. Every flavor of every brand of yogurt she'd ever heard of. Little white cups lined up on her countertop like the foot soldiers of an evil invading army here to destroy her way of life.

Wadding up a plastic sack, he momentarily paused in his deployment of the invading army. Then, once he'd tossed the bag onto the counter and turned his attention to the last sack, he brought out what she knew would be her downfall. The army's secret weapons.

"Mooo Bars?" she challenged.

He looked up. "Yeah. Blue Bell Mooo Bars." His lips quirked into a half smile and she felt her calcium defenses begin to crumble. "I think each ice-cream bar has twenty-five percent of your daily requirement and they're dipped in chocolate, which I knew you'd like." His smile broadened to a full-fledged grin. "And last but not least..." He waved his hand in a flourish as he reached into the bag. "Oreo cookies."

The last of her resistance melted at the sight of the familiar pink packaging. Her throat tightened. "Double-stuffed?"

"Yeah. I thought they'd help with the milk. If you're gonna be drinking three glasses a day, you need something to choke it down with."

She took a step backward, hands raised to ward off the

cookies, bumped into the counter and stumbled over her words. "I don't want those. I can't eat those. Get them away from me."

"What? You don't like Oreo cookies?"

"No! Take them away. The Mooo Bars, too. I don't want them."

"What's wrong with Mooo Bars? They're dipped in chocolate. You like chocolate!"

"What makes you think I like chocolate?"

"You carry Hershey's Kisses in your purse. Besides, I thought all women liked chocolate. It's a hormonal thing."

"Oh, all women like chocolate? Like all women should know how to cook?"

He shrugged, clearly confused. "That's not what I meant."

She pointed an accusing finger at him. "Yes, it is. You said I should cook. Because I'm a woman, right?"

"No, because you're an adult."

"Well, I don't want to cook." Tabitha felt the last of her control slip away. "I don't want to eat Mooo Bars and Oreo cookies. I don't want to be a ma'am or a mother."

"Okay, okay," he murmured. He approached her with raised hands, the way he would a wounded animal or an armed criminal. "Then what do you want?"

"I want to be like the Amazon woman with the bread," she wailed.

In that moment Sam realized how out of control the situation was. One minute he'd been calmly putting away groceries. The next, a crazy pregnant woman was waving her fists at him and ranting about the Amazons. And his sister wondered why he wasn't married yet.

"Okay, Tabitha. Just calm down," he said, only because he didn't have any idea what else to do.

"Calm?" She stepped forward, clutching his shirt in her fists. Tears glistened in her deep blue eyes and her normally porcelain skin turned a blotchy red. "How can I be calm? My life is falling apart! I'm pregnant! And unmarried! And now you want me to start cooking and eating Oreo cookies? Before I know it, I'll gain forty pounds, only ten of which will be baby. I'll be one of those women who sits around watching reruns on TV, talking about how she never has any energy anymore. Or worse, I'll be one of those desperate, peppy women who wear a lot of spandex and try to stay fun and hip even though they're over the hill." She gasped. The red blotches faded to white. "I'll be my mother! I'm turning into my mother and you want me to be calm?"

Panic-stricken by her strange behavior, Sam did the only thing he could think of to do. He pulled her into an embrace. To his surprise, she let him.

"It'll be okay, Tabitha. I promise it'll be okay." *Please, dear God, let this be the right thing to do,* he prayed silently.

For a moment she stood stiffly within the loose circle of his arms. Oh God, he'd been wrong! Any second now she was going to pull back and whop him on the head. Or box him on the ears the way his grandma used to.

He was still trying to figure how he could pretend he'd been reaching for something behind her when she leaned into him and clamped her arms around his waist. Breathing a sigh of relief, he settled his arms against her back. She burrowed her face in his chest and he was surprised by how well she fit against him with the crown of her head tucked under his chin.

He'd never held her before. They'd worked together for more than two years now, and he'd never had occasion to hold her in his arms. No slow dances at station holiday parties. No congratulatory hugs when the ratings went up. She'd hugged other people on the morning show. He had, also, for that matter. But they'd studiously avoided sharing the intimacy of an embrace.

He dismissed carrying her the time she'd been sick. An embrace wasn't an embrace when the female half of it was semiconscious.

Was it an embrace when the female half was semihysterical?

Her arms tightened around him and he could feel the spots where each of her fingers pressed against his back.

Yes, he decided. *When it felt this good, it was definitely an embrace.*

But all this time, he'd avoided holding her in his arms. Now he knew why.

She felt like heaven—warm, curved in all the right places, and just a breath away from not quite being real. She sank against him, flattening her cheek to his chest. He felt her take in a deep breath, then exhale it on a sigh rife with worries carried alone too long.

Something deep in his chest tightened in response. In that instant he knew he'd been kidding himself about his feelings for her. He wasn't helping her just because it was the nice thing to do. He wasn't even helping her because they were partners. He was helping her simply because he didn't want her to go through this alone. He wanted to protect her.

And that made Tabitha a very dangerous woman.

For a second he felt a familiar dread settle over him, a sort of claustrophobic vertigo. As if the fruit and vegetables on the wallpaper were closing in on him, squeezing the very air out of his lungs.

He slammed his eyes closed. One hysterical person was enough for any situation.

He searched his mind for something that might distract her. "Most women turn into their mothers at some point. What's so bad about that?"

He felt her stiffen. She leaned back enough to shoot him a "you're crazy" look. "Have you met my mother?"

"Yeah, last year. She was on the show. Took us all out to lunch afterward. I thought she was fun."

He expected her to step away, but she didn't. Instead she dropped her head back to his shoulder, her deep sigh brushing against his throat, a lock of ebony hair fluttering against his skin.

"Fun? Party hats are fun. Trips to Disneyland are fun. And I suppose as a guest DJ on a radio show, my mom might be fun. But as a mother?" He felt her shake her head against his shoulder. "As mother, she was impossible. She's childish and irresponsible."

"Hey, it can't be that bad."

This time she did step back, giving herself just enough room to gesture emphatically as she said, "She named me after a character from a TV show. She tried to bribe the Girl Scout troop into letting me back in after I got kicked out because she started the fire that burned down all of Camp Woolitaki. The IRS audited her five times while I was growing up. We used to have cookie picnics for dinner. Fig Newtons as a salad, because they're fruity. Nutter Butter cookies for the main course, because they're high in protein. And Oreo cookies for dessert."

"That doesn't sound so bad."

"Once in while, maybe. But every week?"

"Most kids would love that."

"Well, I did, too. Until we studied the four food groups in the third grade and I was the only kid in Mrs. Wexler's class who thought Fig Newtons were a vegetable."

He didn't mean to laugh, especially since she sounded so serious, but a chuckle escape despite his best efforts.

She must have recognized the strangled sound for what it was because she responded, "Sure it makes an amusing anecdote, but I assure you it was quite emotionally scarring to a nine-year-old."

"What did your dad think about all this?"

"I don't know. I guess there wasn't much he could do from a thousand miles away."

"I didn't know your parents were divorced."

"They weren't. They never got married."

Puzzle pieces clicked into place. No wonder she was frantic to get Bob's ring on her finger. He nodded. "I see."

"It's not what you think."

"What?"

"You're thinking the only reason I want to marry Bob is because my parents weren't married. But it's not like that. He would have married her. When he found out she was pregnant, he wanted to get married and move back to Wisconsin where he could work for his father. She said no. She thought marriage would crush her free spirit." She shrugged. "Or maybe it was Wisconsin she objected to. I was never clear on that. He visited when he could. As much to see her as to see us, I think. They always seemed so happy to see each other, but, within hours, they'd be at one another's throat. Then one visit he realized she was never going to marry him and he just stopped coming. I didn't blame him. She made him miserable."

She was silent for a long minute and he thought she wasn't going to say anything else, but finally she spoke. "It's ironic. All my life, all I ever wanted was to *not* be like her. And here I am...pregnant and unmarried. And eating Oreo cookies."

He wanted to pull her back into his arms. He tried to

tell himself it was just because she looked so forlorn, but he was afraid it had nothing to do with that and everything to do with how good her body felt held against his.

But he didn't pull her back into the embrace—it was bad enough he'd done it the first time. Instead he reached out and trapped a stray curl between his fingers. He held it for just a second, noticing for the first time how soft, how alive, her hair seemed. He carefully tucked the curl behind her ear, then met her gaze.

"If you're worried about being like your mother... don't. You're not like her. You're not irresponsible. You're not childish. And if anyone can handle single motherhood, you can. You're the most together woman I know."

Her eyes widened as he spoke and once again tears welled in them. She blinked rapidly and swallowed before offering up a tremulous smile. "That's not saying much." Her lips twisted into a wry smile. "Sam?"

"Yeah?" *Okay, here it comes. This is where she slaps my face and lectures me on workplace familiarity and sexual harassment.*

Instead she bit her lip and broadened her smile. "I'm not gonna freak out again."

He raised an eyebrow. "You sure?"

She nodded, stepped back and leaned her hip against the opposite counter. "Yeah." She used both hands to smooth down her hair, then wiped at her cheeks with the backs of her fingers. "See? All better now."

Her voice sounded strong, but he noticed her hands trembled as she tucked them into her back pockets. Her lips wavered in their smile and she swallowed before speaking again.

"I'm sorry about this." She waved a hand back and

forth between them. "Damn pregnancy hormones. It won't happen again."

"Well, if you ever need another shoulder to lean on, I'm your man." Her head tilted to one side and she eyed him speculatively. Something sparked in her eyes, something hot and vital. Something he'd never seen before but that he knew could bring him to his knees. "I, um, meant for...crying purposes only. You know, I've heard pregnant women...cry...a lot."

She nodded, but that curious look didn't leave her eyes. Definitely time to exit stage left.

"I should...be going. Now." He gestured at the door and started backing toward it.

"Is something wrong?"

"No." He must have answered a bit too quickly because she took a step toward him. He grabbed the bag of Oreos and held it up, like a vampire's victim clasping crossed toothpicks. "Should I take the cookies? And the Mooo Bars?"

That stopped her dead in her tracks. She considered for a moment. "No," she said with a sigh of resignation. Whatever look had been in her eyes had been replaced by concern. Or he'd imagined it. Either way, it didn't matter. "Better leave them. The Mooo Bars would melt before you got them home anyway."

He thrust the package into her hands and all but dashed for the door. He'd almost made it to freedom when he stopped. He turned to find Tabitha had followed him into the living room.

With his hand resting on the doorknob as if it were a lifeline, he cautiously broached the subject that had kept him from escaping while he'd had the chance. "After this afternoon, don't you think you should talk to Marty about this ridiculous contest?"

Her spine straightened and he could tell he'd crossed the line from supportive friend back to meddlesome co-worker.

"No, I don't. I told Marty I'd do it. The station would look bad if I backed out now. Besides, it's harmless."

"Bullshit. It's added stress, which you don't need right now."

"It's only stressful because you're making such a big deal out of it. Besides, it's only a couple of weeks and then I'll have my life back. I can put up with anything for a couple of weeks."

4

"HEY, MAN, you want to hear my letter?"

Sam glanced from the beer in his hand to the man seated across from him. So this was why he'd been invited in for a beer. He'd been suspicious from the start.

Newton Doyle rented the other half of Sam's divided Victorian house. He'd bought the dinosaur years ago, thinking he might someday renovate it back into a single-family home. In the meantime, the extra rent from the other half didn't hurt.

Newt was a good guy, despite his odd appearance. He had a tall, lean frame and a shock of red hair, cropped close on the sides and long on top so it poofed up.

They hung out sometimes, but Newt, like many computer programmers, worked long and odd hours. Days or even weeks could go by without Newt even leaving the house. Usually only a major sporting event or a Star Trek convention could lure him out. Even now, a trash bag full of soda cans sat in the corner and the aroma of stale pizza hung in the air as testament to his most recent working binge.

But today, when Newt had stopped him on the walkway to invite him in for a beer, he'd jumped at the chance. Mostly because, after Tabitha's bout of hysteria, he felt the need for a little uncomplicated male company. And now this.

"No. I don't want to hear your letter. I want to drink

my beer." He gestured with the half-empty bottle. "It wouldn't do you any good anyway. Tabitha picks them, not me."

Newt leaned forward. The office chair in which he sat let loose a series of creaks and groans in protest. "Yeah, yeah. I know. I just thought you could see if she'd like it, since you know her. Here."

Newt thrust the paper forward, leaving Sam little choice but to take it.

Sam set down his beer and unfolded the letter. He owed the guy that much. After all, every time his computer crashed, Newt came over to resuscitate it.

When he glanced down, the phrase "throbbing masculinity" jumped out at him. He jerked his gaze back up to his friend. "Jeez, Newt, where'd you get this?"

"Good, huh? Isn't it?" Newt rolled his chair until it bumped the computer desk behind him. He spun the chair around and grabbed a stack of books and spread them out on the floor between them. Some of the covers featured Georgia O'Keeffe-ish flowers, others pictured couples locked in embraces.

"I figured women like romance novels, right? So I spent the past two days scanning the top-five romance novels from each of the past three years. Then I wrote a program that analyzed the books and wrote the letter for me." Newt leaned forward, again torturing the chair. "It's good, right? She'll like it?"

"You spent two days on this? I thought you had some big deadline."

"Oh, yeah. The big conference. Three weeks." Newt waved a dismissive hand. "But I figured, hey, this is my chance, man. Tabitha would never look twice at me, but if I can send a really great letter, then I'll have my foot in the door. I'll get to meet her when I pick up my T-shirt. Maybe she'll pick me for the date."

For a moment Sam could only stare at Newt. The anger knotting his stomach surprised him. Surely he wasn't angry at Newt just because he had a crush on Tabitha. Hell, if the number of letters flooding the station was any indication, half the damn town had a crush on her. The knot in his stomach tightened. He squelched the sensation.

"Let me see if I've got this right," he said, leaning forward to rest his elbows on his knees. "You've been working on this program for two years, living off pizza and doughnuts. In three weeks you're supposed to unveil this miracle product that's gonna revolutionize the gaming industry, and you took a couple of days off to come up with this?" He held up the letter.

Newt's nod was eager, as if he couldn't see the absurdity of his own behavior. Sam could only turn his attention back to the letter. Maybe the rest of it would be better than the first line. It wasn't.

"So? What do you think?"

Sam put down the letter, ignoring the urge to wash his hands. "Newt, when you scanned in those romance novels, did you scan in the whole thing?"

"No. That would have taken too long. I scanned in just the sex scenes 'cause that's where the romance is, right?"

"The sex scenes are where the sex is. Not the romance."

"What? You don't think she'll like it?" Newt's brow furrowed in confusion.

"It reads like a letter to *Penthouse.*"

Newt sat back in his chair. After a moment he nodded slowly and said only, "Oh."

It was grim indeed when Newt could be reduced to a one-word response.

After a long moment he asked, "Hey, do girls like *Penthouse?*"

Good question. He knew some women did, but did Tabitha? Maybe tomorrow on the air he'd ask her.

He could picture her response. She'd blush, her cheeks tinging pink with embarrassment. For an instant she'd be flustered. But she'd recover quickly, then shoot him a look of annoyance to hide her embarrassment, before quipping some sassy comeback. He could see it as clearly as if she was sitting with him right now.

What he didn't want was to imagine her response to Newt's letter. Instead of trying to explain or to justify his actions, Sam just shook his head. "No. Usually not."

The desk chair let out a soulful squeal as Newt rotated toward the stack of books and glared accusingly at them. Guilt flooded Sam.

"You really have a thing for her," he observed.

Newt rocked back and forth in his chair in what Sam could only conclude was an affirmative.

The squealing chair grated on his already threadbare nerves, tightening the knot in his stomach. The urge to commit violence, throw the damn chair out the window, for example, surprised him. This sudden, rash anger felt a little like...jealousy.

That thought swept away his anger in a tide of panic. He couldn't be jealous!

Could he?

No. No, definitely not.

And yet... And yet, she had felt good in his arms this afternoon. Surprisingly good. As though she fit. As though she was meant to be there.

For a long moment he considered the possibility. Any

relationship between the two of them was doomed from the start. As he'd told Marie, he just wasn't ready to settle down. And Tabitha was all about settling down. As soon as she realized he wasn't ready to commit—not to her, not to any woman—she'd walk away from him.

They were both professionals. They'd try not to let it affect their work relationship, but it would. In the end, his inability to keep his hands to himself would doom their on-air relationship.

He needed to put a stop to this. And fast. He had never felt jealous when she was involved with Bob. So all he needed to do was hook her up with someone new.

The steady squeak of the chair brought his attention back to Newt. A little odd, maybe, but hell, who wasn't? He was as good as anyone. And darn successful, in his own way. So what if Newt had never had a serious girlfriend? Some women liked that. Okay, he didn't have the social skills some guys had. Tabitha could probably look past that. Couldn't she?

And if she had to have a boyfriend, wouldn't Newt be better than someone socially adept and financially responsible like Bob?

"Look, if you want to write her a letter, you have to do it yourself. You can't write a program to do it for you. You've got to tell her what you like about her. Tell her how you feel."

Newt's expression brightened only slightly. "Ah, man, I can't do that. You know me. I'm not good with words. Besides Tabitha's like...you know." Newt sliced his hand through the air near his head. "And I'm...you know, like..." He waved his other hand much lower. "I mean, I wouldn't even know what to say."

He felt a flood of sympathy for Newt. The poor guy was obviously infatuated with Tabitha and the letter he'd already written…well, it was as likely to get him arrested as it was of getting him close enough to meet her. He pondered the problem for a minute, then drained the last of his beer and sat forward. "Okay. Here's the deal. I'll help you write the letter."

"All right!"

"But you have to understand, I'm only helping with the letter. I can't do anything else for you."

"Okay, okay. That's cool."

In seconds Newt had his computer up and running and was typing in the words "Dear Tabby."

"No, don't call her that. She hates it."

"But that's what you call her on the show."

He shook his head. "Only on the air. And only if I'm trying to piss her off."

Newt backspaced, then typed "Tabitha." "Okay. What now?"

"It's your letter. What do you want to say to her?" Newt looked at him blankly. The silence stretched between them for a long moment before Sam finally relented. "Start by telling her what you like about her."

"Her tits, man. She's got the best pair of—"

"She's my partner. Treat her with a little respect, okay?" Sam cut Newt off before he could even finish the thought. He didn't want to consider that it was the jealousy thing again. He'd put that to rest. Must be the pregnancy thing.

God, he hoped it was the pregnancy thing. He was just feeling protective. After all, she *was* his partner.

"Besides," he continued, "if you put stuff in there about her tits, she'll think you're a loser."

"Oh. Good thinking. Right. Okay. No stuff about her tits. I guess her great ass is out then, too."

"Yeah," Sam said dryly. "Her great ass is definitely

out. Come on, there's got to be something you like about her besides her body. You couldn't have seen her more than once or twice."

"Okay. Okay. I got it." Newt hunched over the keyboard, pecked with his forefingers for a minute then leaned back, a smile on his face.

Sam read out loud from the screen. "'Dear Tabitha, I think you'd make a really great girlfriend because I listen to your show every morning.'" So far, not great, but full of potential. "'I know you must be tolerant, because you put up with so much crap from Sam.'"

Newt nodded in satisfaction, making Sam want to belt him.

Instead he said, "Get up." With one hand, he pulled Newt's chair away from the computer.

"What?" he cried indignantly.

"Let me type. Otherwise we'll never get this done." And where would that leave him? Damn near blind with lust for a woman he couldn't touch, that's where. He had to get Tabitha back into a relationship before this jealousy thing got the better of him.

Newt frowned, but moved from the chair.

With a grim sense of purpose, Sam began typing. "Dear Tabitha, Every morning I wake to the sound of your voice..."

"AFTER THE BREAK, Tabitha will read today's winning love letter. You won't want to miss it—this one's really hot. If it's yours, give us a call within the next fifteen minutes to pick up a limited edition K-O-N-E 'I ♥ Tabitha' T-shirt. Don't go away."

As soon as Sam cued up the commercial, Tabitha slipped back into the booth from her break. With just three minutes to spare, she settled quickly into her chair.

"Thanks for covering for me."

"No problem." As he said the words his gaze dropped to her mouth. "You've got…"

Instead of finishing the sentence he reached over and brushed his thumb across her lower lip. A dusting of saltine crumbs fell onto her lap unnoticed. Heat spiraled through her and she shifted uncomfortably under his gaze.

Don't be silly, she told herself. Repressing a shiver, she wiped at her mouth with the back of her hand, then licked her lips.

"Look, Sam. I wanted to thank you for the other day." Her stomach flopped over at the memory of being held in his arms. Suddenly nervous, she picked up the stack of papers in front of her and squared them on the desk. "I…"

But her voice faded as she noticed the paper on top of the stack.

A few minutes ago when she'd left for the rest room, the top page had been the letter she'd chosen to read today. A complimentary, if rather bland note from a single father.

Now the bland letter was gone. In its place was the one letter she never wanted to read on the air.

"Tabitha, you're on in ten."

Her head jerked up at the sound of Sam's voice. She looked around, then frantically flipped through the papers for her single-dad letter. For any other letter.

Then her gaze caught Jasmine's. Jasmine shifted nervously, refusing to maintain eye contact. Through her headphones, she heard the last few seconds of the commercial, then she was cued in.

She hesitated only a second before launching into the spiel Marty had written for her to promote the contest.

Marty's hook bought her a little time. Time she used to tap into her memory, hoping she might remember enough of the single-dad letter to wing it. But in the end, only one letter stood out in her mind. This letter.

She clutched the single page in her hands as she finished reading Marty's scripted words. "Don't forget, you still have two weeks to get your letters in." By rote, she dropped her voice a notch. "I'm waiting to hear from you. Let's see if you can top this one..."

Taking in a deep breath, she looked down at the paper. The letter was printed on a single sheet of high-quality computer paper. One of the fancy cotton blends. Beneath her fingertips, it felt like the finest vellum.

Slowly she began to read. "'Dear Tabitha, Every morning I wake to the sound of your voice.'" She almost didn't have to look at the page to read it out loud, the words were etched so deeply on her soul. "'Even if I'm already out of bed and going about my day, I don't feel human until I hear you say the words 'Good morning, Austin.'

"'Some mornings only the lure of your voice can coax me from sleep. Those are the mornings I lie there, eyes closed, and pretend you're talking to me. Just me. I imagine you're not on the radio. No one's paying you to talk to me. This is more than just a job for you. It's me who's made you laugh. Me who's made your face light up with a smile. Please, Tabitha, give me the chance to meet you. To make you smile for me.'"

She exhaled slowly, but it did little to quiet the butterflies in her stomach. After a heartbeat she continued. "That wonderful letter was written by Newton Doyle. Newton, if you're listening, give me a call here at the studio and I'll see about getting you your free T-shirt."

The rest of the show passed in a blur. Luckily, Sam was rocking and he picked up her slack. By the time she stumbled out of the booth at ten o'clock, she graduated from stunned daze to righteous anger.

Jasmine had barely made it into the hall when Tabitha pinned her verbally against wall. "You went through my desk."

The other woman blinked innocently. "I don't know what you're talking about."

"This—" Tabitha waved the letter in front of her "—was not the letter I picked to read."

"Well, it should have been." Jasmine propped her hands on her hips and bumped up her chin defiantly. "It's much better than that insipid thing you picked."

"But it was the letter *I'd* picked. You had no right to go through my things." She poked the air with the folded letter to make her point.

Jasmine snatched the letter from Tabitha's fingers. "As if I have time to dig through your stuff. I stopped by your desk on the way down to lunch yesterday to see if you had that new ad for the electronics store. This was right on top. I picked it up by accident." She clutched it to her chest. "It's such a great letter. You can't blame me for wanting you to read it."

Tabitha narrowed her eyes. "This letter was at the bottom of a stack of fifty. In a file folder. In my desk. Which I locked."

Jasmine didn't even blush with shame. "Oh, please. Like you've never gone through my desk."

"I've *never* gone through your desk."

"Not even looking for chocolate?"

The little snipe had her there. She eyed Jasmine for a moment before finally owning up. "Just that one time last January. I was going through post-Christmas withdrawal. And that has nothing to do with this."

"Of course it does. You can't be mad at me when

you've done the same thing. And I was looking for the
new ad. Besides, you're only in such a snit about me
snooping, because you're hoping I'll forget about the letter. As if I could." Jasmine fanned herself with her hand.

"Fine. You went through my desk and found the letter.
That doesn't explain how it ended up in the booth this
morning."

"What's wrong?"

Tabitha turned in time to see Sam approaching. Since
the Mooo Bar and Oreo debacle at her house, she'd been
avoiding him when they weren't on the air. Even on the
air, when she was supposed to be working, she found her
mind drifting back to that day. To how strong his arms
had felt around her. To how the beat of his heart had echoed in her memory long after she'd lifted her head from
his chest.

Today his lips were curved in a self-satisfied smile that
held just a hint of knee-weakening arrogance.

And why shouldn't he be satisfied? The show had
gone well today and it was all due to him. She'd dropped
the ball and he'd caught it. Their ability to compensate
for one another was part of made them such a great team,
but it irked her that she hadn't been at the top of her
game today. All because of some stupid letter.

"What's up?" he asked again.

Great. She'd been caught staring at him like some sort
of mute idiot. Just great. "Jasmine and I were just dis-
cussing—"

"Tabitha's pissed because I'm being pushy."

"—something private," she finished lamely.

"Pushy, huh? What'd you do?"

"She'd picked some boring letter to read today." Jasmine rolled her eyes. "I found a better one and replaced
it while she was in the bathroom. You know, when I

snuck in while she was gone? That's when I switched the letters."

Sam's self-satisfied grin dimmed as he turned to her. "You didn't pick the letter you read?"

"No."

"What? You didn't like it?"

She studied him, surprised he'd ask. "I just..." *Loved the letter.*

But she hadn't wanted to share it with all of Austin. How could she explain that to Sam and Jasmine when she didn't understand it herself?

She found herself lying to cover how much she did like it. "It was okay, I suppose. Certainly nothing special."

Jasmine threw up her hands in a gesture of dramatic disbelief. "Oh, come on! Newton Doyle's letter is brilliant. Perfect."

Tabitha snorted. "Hardly." Okay, she didn't want to overdo it. "I mean, perfect is a bit of an exaggeration."

Jasmine flipped open the page and scanned it. "He sounds so into you. I wonder if he's someone you know. Do you know anyone named Newton?"

"Nope."

"Well, it's really romantic." Jasmine turned to Sam. "What do you think?"

Sam's smile flattened into a frown. Plucking the letter from Jasmine's fingers, he stared at it, his expression blank. "She's right. It's no work of art." He tossed it back toward Tabitha. "Just some idiot rambling on."

"But the listeners loved it!" Jasmine protested. "We got more calls about this letter than any other."

He shrugged. "Hey, whatever's good for the ratings."

Stung by his brutal reminder that this was all about the ratings, Tabitha snapped, "Is that all you care about?"

"We don't have jobs if we don't get ratings. It's all any

of us should care about. And you're the one who agreed to the contest. Don't bitch about it now."

"Thanks, Sam. That's very helpful." Fuming, she stalked off.

"Hey, wait up!" Jasmine called from behind her.

Tabitha didn't even slow down. Jasmine caught up with her half a dozen steps down the hall. When she looked over her shoulder, she noticed Sam hadn't moved but was watching them, his face etched with a scowl.

What had pissed him off?

Humph. Men.

Shaking her head, she turned to face Jasmine, who beamed innocently at her.

Humph. Women.

"I don't even want to talk to you."

Jasmine shot her a droll look. "You're lucky you've got me to look out for you."

"Lucky? Lucky that I've got you to meddle in my business? I don't think so."

"Yes, lucky. If it wasn't for me, you never would have read Newton Doyle's letter on the air."

"That was the general idea," she said.

"But," Jasmine countered, "if you hadn't read the letter, you never would have had the opportunity to meet him."

Tabitha halted her feet, frozen by shock. "Meet him. I can't meet him."

"Of course you can. When he comes to pick up his T-shirt, you'll be here. You can meet him. And if you like him, you pick his letter as the grand-prize winner and then you'll get to go out with him."

Her heartbeat raced at the thought, but reason overruled her body's enthusiasm. "So the guy writes a nice letter. Don't make a big deal out of it."

"But it is a big deal. This guy must really like you. And you need to get back out there."

"Isn't that why I agreed to date the mini food processor?"

"Well, sure, but Newton sounds like a real blender." She sighed dramatically.

Glancing back over her shoulder toward where Sam had stood just moments ago, she mused, "Right now another blender is the last thing I need."

Jasmine followed her gaze. "What? Sam? You think Sam is a blender?"

He'd certainly had her churned up.

"It doesn't matter what Sam is," she said. "Besides, today he's more of a mystery than anything else."

"Forget about Sam. Newton Doyle is just the guy to get you back into the race."

If only forgetting Sam was that easy. But whether she managed to put Sam out of her mind or not, she wasn't going to date Newton Doyle. "No, he's not."

"Why not?"

"Well, to begin with, he's a listener. I'm not Sam. I don't date listeners."

"You should. Our listeners are great. If you ask me, that was one of Bob's problems. Never trust a man under forty who tunes in exclusively to the easy-listening station."

"Second..." She had to rack her brain to come up with a second. Finally it came to her. But she didn't like it any more than Jasmine would. In a much less enthusiastic tone, she continued. "Second, Newton Doyle could be anyone. He could be a twelve-year-old boy or a ninety-year-old lech. He could be married or in jail. We don't know anything about this person. I can't go out on a date with someone I don't even know."

"You've already agreed to go out on one date with a complete stranger. It's part of the contest. Why not choose Newton Doyle?"

Why not, indeed.

The sad truth was Newton Doyle sounded like a great guy, which was the last thing she needed in her life right now.

In thirty-two weeks she would be knee-deep in diapers. It wouldn't be fair to try to start a relationship with that looming in her immediate future. Some tiny part of her wished she could be the kind of woman who would run out and have all the fun she could now, while she was still free. But the truth was, she was no longer the woman with the French bread and the wine. She was the woman with the prenatal vitamins and the binge food in her cart.

God help her.

She turned to face Jasmine. "Look, I said I'd go out on one blind date with a listener and I will. But just one. I have no intention of letting that date lead to anything other than what my contract stipulates. I'll pick someone boring and predictable and have one boring, predictable date with that person."

"But—"

"No." She cut off Jasmine's protests with a wave of her hand. "I'll say this only once. There's nothing in the world that could make me go out with Newton Doyle."

5

"ANY IDEAS WHO you're going to pick for your big date?" Sam asked, looking at her over the rim of his coffee mug.

"I'm narrowing it down, I think." Unsure what to make of his question—or his behavior, for that matter—Tabitha shrugged, then brought the cup of hot chocolate to her lips.

She didn't know why he'd insisted on taking her out for coffee after work. She didn't know why she'd accepted. And she didn't know why the thought of being with Sam made her blood hotter than the chocolately treat she was sipping.

Since he'd found out about her pregnancy, Sam's behavior had ranged from baffling to outright bizarre. The only thing more confusing than his behavior was her own.

Lately, even the sound of his voice sent her thoughts in inappropriate directions. Just watching him drink coffee was torture. So instead she pretended to study the coffee shop. From a brief glance, the place seemed like a dump with its cheap Formica-topped tables and fifties-style chairs.

The tables and chairs were small, downsized to fit the intimate atmosphere. The furniture emphasized Sam's bulky frame. Under their table, his knees brushed against hers and every time she reached for her mug, his hands seemed in the way.

He set down his coffee. "So, which of the letters have you liked?"

"Why do you care? You think the contest is stupid."

"Just curious." He shrugged. "For the record, the contest is stupid."

"Actually, I'm enjoying it. It's a chance to meet new people."

"Give me a break."

"No, really. After all, you've had luck dating listeners."

"What's that supposed to mean?"

"Come on, Sam, you've dated dozens of listeners."

"I have?"

"Oh, yeah."

"Dozens?"

"Well, at least a dozen."

He raised an eyebrow speculatively. "Tell you what, if you can name twelve listeners I've dated in the past two years, I won't say another word about the contest."

"There have been at least half a dozen blondes alone."

"Name them."

"Okay, I will. First there was Shelby, the waitress. Then there was Suzy, the dancer. Julie, the librarian. And—"

"Julie wasn't a listener."

"What?"

"Julie didn't listen to the radio. She was deaf."

"Oh." She paused, momentarily thrown off her stride. "I didn't know that. How did you meet a deaf librarian?"

"At the library."

"You go to the library?"

"Your confidence in my intellect is inspiring," he muttered.

"Sorry. I just didn't picture you as the library type."

"You know, Tabitha, you don't know me as well as you think you do." He gulped down some coffee and added, "That's two so far, Shelby and Suzy. Who else have you got?"

Tabitha took a sip of hot chocolate to hide the blank she was suddenly drawing. Only two? She knew, just knew, he'd dated more women than that in the two years she'd known him. Finally she set down her cup and announced, "The brunette."

"Huh?"

"The first month I worked here there was a little brunette who used to come to all the remotes."

"Debbie?"

"Right. Debbie."

"I never dated Debbie."

"Of course you did. She hung out around you all the time."

"No, I really didn't. She was Josh's fiancée. That's why she came to all the remotes."

"Josh? Who's Josh?"

"The guy who used to do Jasmine's job. Left a couple of weeks after we hired you. I can't believe you don't remember Josh."

"You can't expect me to remember everybody I meet."

"But you thought you could remember every woman I've dated in the past two years?"

"Not every woman. Just twelve of them. I'm not a genius."

"You're not gonna remember twelve of them, because I haven't dated twelve women in the past two years."

"Are you sure?"

"Yeah, I'm sure." He chuckled. "Jeez, life with Bob must've been pretty boring if you'd had this much time to keep track of what I was doing."

She sank a little farther down in the chair and glared at him over the edge of her mug. Why *had* she spent so much energy obsessing about Sam's girlfriends? Was life with Bob really that boring?

Or was Sam just that interesting?

"Fine. But my original point is still valid. You've gotten along great with the listeners you've dated."

"Right, both of them."

"There was that other woman…what was her name? The one you brought to last year's Christmas party?"

"Rachel?"

"Yeah, Rachel. You two seemed to have a lot in common."

"All we had in common was that we both liked to have sex in semipublic places."

She choked on her mouthful of hot chocolate, nearly spewing it all over Sam. Luckily she brought her throat muscles back under control and swallowed.

Sex in semipublic places. Sam having sex in semipublic places. She'd never even thought of doing something so…uninhibited. Obviously, Sam had.

And apparently he'd not only thought of it, he'd taken that little fantasy out for a test drive. The thought gave her pause.

How often? And where? What did semipublic mean? Elevators? Public restrooms? Or something even more public?

She set down her mug and leaned back in the chair, praying the coffee shop was too dark for him to see the blush she could feel working its way up her neck. And her face wasn't the only part of her that felt suddenly hot. Not by a long run.

One look at Sam told her that no amount of poor lighting could hide her blush. He was giving her that smile of his. The same one he wore whenever he said something particularly shocking on the air. It was a mischievous, secretive, sexy little grin. And it sent her blood pumping, her breath whooshing right out of her lungs, and her imagination running like an Olympic sprinter.

Before she could get a handle on it, her devious little mind had conjured up an image of Sam's nearly naked body pressing some woman against the office wall. And since, for the life of her, she couldn't remember what that Rachel woman looked like, the woman in the fantasy bore a striking resemblance to herself.

Sam's grin broadened, almost as if he'd read her mind. "I've shocked you," he murmured.

No, she'd shocked herself. And now she had another Sam fantasy to add to her repertoire, as if she needed any more Sam fantasies.

And frankly, in her condition, she had no business fantasizing about anyone, except maybe Bob.

But try as she might, she couldn't conjure up a single smoldering vision of Bob. Nothing she tried made her mind replace Sam's low-slung jeans with Bob's practical Dockers. Or Sam's tousled hair with Bob's ash-blond crew cut. Or Sam's finely muscled bare back with Bob's pasty, pale one.

Well, darn it. There was the problem. Bob simply lacked sex appeal. She'd known that when they started dating. All these years she'd been okay with his lack of sex appeal. She'd been okay with his pasty back and his unimaginative, once-a-week, always-in-bed sex. Now, all of sudden, she wanted a muscular back and sex up against the wall of an elevator. Or even her own living room wall, right in front of that big picture window.

Oh, dear.

What had come over her? Was this some weird side effect of the pregnancy?

She made a mental note to check her copy of *What to Expect When You're Expecting* for any mention of bizarre, out-of-character sexual urges.

She didn't want Sam to see he'd sparked her interest. Better to put him on the defensive.

With sultry bravado she said, "No, you haven't shocked me at all. How do you know I'm not an exhibitionist myself?"

His jaw dropped a fraction of an inch. Then he snapped it closed and swallowed. His dazed expression satisfied her.

Then his face cleared and he shook his head and smiled. Then he laughed. Out loud.

"What?" She straightened. "What's so funny?"

"With Bob? You want me to believe you're an exhibitionist with Bob? I can't imagine him having sex with his socks off, let alone in a public place." He chuckled. "Nice try, though. You had me going for a second."

She fumed. "For all you know, Bob was wild in bed."

"If Bob had been even a little wild, I'd be a lot less worried about this contest."

Annoyed at her own overheated imagination, she snapped, "Oh, stop harping on the contest. You're starting to sound like a jealous boyfriend. It doesn't become you."

As quickly as she had blushed, Sam paled. "I'm not jealous!" He tried to soften the exclamation with a smirk. "Why would I be jealous? I'm not your boyfriend." The false smirk faded to a dull, panicked expression. "Bob's the one who should be jealous."

She stared at him in confusion for a second before his

words sank in. Then she jerked forward in her chair, gesturing with both hands. "Sam, you're a genius!"

"I am?"

"Yes, you are! You definitely are! The date will make Bob jealous. It'll be advertised all over town. I'll pick someone handsome and successful and then talk about it on the radio. He's sure to hear about it. And when he does, his overwhelming jealousy will drive him back to me."

And with Bob back in her life, she could regain control of her attraction to Sam. She might not be able to squash her desire for him completely, but at least she'd be able to banish him to the occasional fantasy.

It was a strategic maneuver worthy of a four-star general. Now all she needed were the troops—scratch that, the contest winner.

6

"CANDLELIGHT. Soft music. Starry skies." Tabitha leaned low over the microphone, speaking slowly, as if she were savoring every word.

God knows, he was. Odd, how lately just the sound of her voice got his blood pumping.

"Sitting in front of an old brick fireplace, sipping a fine red wine..."

This was her show. He didn't want anything to do with it.

"Or a big mug of hot chocolate, topped with whipped cream." She paused, glancing in his direction. Feigning disinterest, he nodded as he rocked back in his chair.

She shifted in her seat, turning ever so slightly away from him. He could see only her profile. She continued talking in the huskiest, most seductive version of her radio voice.

"Real silk stockings, the kind that slip and shimmer over a woman's legs."

Surprised by her words, Sam let his chair drop forward and spun to face her. He cocked his head to get a look at her legs. She wore a simple knee-length dress, but since she was seated, the hem bisected her thigh, exposing most of her slender—silk encased?—legs.

He swallowed.

She ignored him and went on. "Skinny-dipping on a moonlit night. Or maybe something more public." She paused, letting the implication hang in the air. "Two-stepping across an old oak floor, while a slow, sexy ballad plays in the background.

"What do you think is romantic? What's your dream date? If you're single, if you know how a woman wants to be treated, then you're the man I want to hear from." As she spoke, her lips curved in a hint of a smile. Damn, she was enjoying this.

"Write it down. Spell it out. Every moment. Every luscious, decadent detail, because I'm in the mood to be spoiled. To be charmed. To be romanced."

She let the last word hang in the air for a moment before easing back in her seat and looking in Sam's direction. Her lips curved into a smile. He'd seen cats lick cream off their whiskers with less satisfaction. He stared back at her, still reeling.

Slowly, she leaned back to her microphone and murmured, "Apparently, Sam needs a moment to get himself together. Sam, honey, you just let me know when you're ready."

Oh, crap. He'd missed his cue. Embarrassment washed over him like a wave of cold water as he spoke into his microphone. "When we get back, we'll have all the information about the 5-K Run for AIDS Services of Austin. But first, we've got the song everybody wants to hear, 'Unforgettable.' So don't go away."

He cued up the music. In seconds the sensual thrum filled the booth. A glance across the equipment at Tabitha took his breath away.

Her eyes drifted closed as she swayed gently to the rhythm of the song. She brushed back her hair, unconsciously moving in time to the singer's throaty praise of her lover.

He'd never hear that song without thinking of her.

Without picturing her as she looked in this instant, head tilted back, neck exposed, lips moist and parted. Her pure visceral pleasure stirred him in a way even her earlier words hadn't. And that was saying a lot.

As the song ended Tabitha sighed and stretched languidly. Slowly she eased her eyes opened. He cued up the commercial and spun back to face her.

Before he could say a word, she blinked rapidly as if waking. Then she leaned forward in his chair, her head tilted in concern, and asked, "Are you all right?"

"What?"

"You look a little pale."

Right. A little pale. That was probably because the blood had stopped flowing to his brain. Just watching her tied him in knots. She was making him crazy.

Which was exactly what she'd intended. She wanted to drive him crazy. Him and every other guy in the metroplex, he realized with a surge of jealousy. "I'm fine."

No. Not jealousy, he told himself. Concern. Just concern. Nothing as proprietary as jealousy. Still he couldn't seem to help demanding, "What the hell was that?"

"What?" she asked innocently.

"Skinny-dipping?" He sat forward, propping his elbows on his knees and clenching his fists. "Skinnydipping! Are you crazy?"

"What? You're not one of those guys who's afraid of microbes in water, are you?"

"Microbes? No—"

She frowned. "Then what? You don't think skinnydipping is sexy?"

"Are you looking for a date or just encouraging the neighborhood stalker?"

She looked genuinely disturbed. "Stalker? Of course not! I wanted something provocative, enticing." She slumped back in her chair in defeat. She absentmindedly nibbled on one of her thumbnails and traced the base of the microphone with the forefinger of her other hand. "I thought it sounded good last night when I was working on it, but I should have known I wouldn't be able to pull it off."

He almost laughed out loud at her obvious dejection. "Honey, it wasn't that—" But he cut himself off. What would it hurt if she thought she hadn't pulled it off? So, it would bruise her ego a little. She'd get over it.

He leaned forward, placing a comforting hand over hers. "Look, you can still back out of this."

Her eyes met his, dejected but not defeated, and she jerked her hand out from under his. "I'm sure you'd like that. But no, thank you. Maybe I did sound stupid, but this is still my best bet for making Bob jealous."

"It's a stupid idea."

She turned, glaring at him. "It's not a stupid idea. It'll work."

"Why would you want that loser?"

"Because he's the father of my child, that's why."

"He's the guy who got you pregnant. That doesn't mean he's going to be a good father."

"Look, I know you pride yourself on flaunting convention, but I don't. I know what it's like to grow up without a father. I don't want that for my child."

"Bob isn't the only man who can be a good father to your child."

"I'm sure that's exactly what my mom thought every time she brought home a new boyfriend. But they never stuck around. They never cared about us enough to stay longer than a few months."

"It doesn't have to be like that. You might meet someone else—" his throat inexplicably tightened at the thought, and he had to force out the last of his sentence "—that you want to marry."

She pinned him with a critical stare. "Right. Because the streets are overflowing with single men who can't wait to be stepfathers. I hear all the time about how single mothers have to beat off men with a stick."

"Are the streets overflowing with men like that? No. But they are out there. My stepfather was great."

"Your mom didn't marry him until you were nineteen. He only had to be a great stepfather for a couple of years."

"To me, maybe. But Marie and Lizzy were still kids. He raised them." He found himself smiling, somehow relieved Tabitha wasn't in a rush to get involved with some new guy. "Besides, you have no idea how much trouble I was as a teenager."

Her lips quirked upward in a delectable grin. "Sam, you're always trouble."

There was a twinkle in her gaze that sent his blood spinning.

Before he could think of a response, he heard Jasmine's voice on the headset. "Heads up, you two. You're on in ten."

Crap! The second time today he'd forgotten to do his job. He shot Tabitha a look he hoped told her the discussion wasn't over, and then spun around in his chair to face his microphone, determined to think of something to convince her to call off this date contest. Before she was inundated with the wet dreams of every loser in the city.

TABITHA ONLY half listened to Sam. The other half of her mind was firmly focused on what he'd said during the break. He hadn't liked the way she'd pitched the contest. Fine.

She wasn't a vamp or a siren. She was more the girl-next-door type. The girl guys respected. The boring one. And if, for one brief moment, she'd forgotten that, well, that was Newton Doyle's fault.

The letter he'd sent her last week had made her feel...irresistible. And maybe just a little vampish. But she could only blame Newton Doyle for so much. Because if she'd gotten a kick out of pitching the contest, if she'd glanced over at Sam and sensed her words had sparked his interest, and if she'd felt a little shiver of anticipation in response, well then, that was her fantasy and no one else's.

She glanced over at Sam. He'd segued from the commercial break into the next song without her even noticing. Absentmindedly, she flipped through her notes. After the next song Sam was supposed to ask listeners to call in and talk about their pets' names. Not the most exciting topic of conversation, but she figured they would get lots of calls. People liked to talk about their lives.

She forced herself to sit up a little straighter and refocus her attention on the show. Once listeners started responding, Sam would need her to pull her own weight.

She was still listening with only half an ear when Sam said, "I've got a question for all you poor saps stuck in traffic right now, a little something to think about. Fatherhood."

She snapped her head around to look at Sam. Fatherhood? What was he talking about? She tried to catch his eye so she could shoot him a questioning look, but he didn't so much as glance her way.

"Fatherhood," he said again into the microphone. "What does it take to be a good father?"

Once again she scanned her notes, even though she knew they hadn't planned to talk about fatherhood. She abandoned her attempts at discretion and tried to cut him off. "Sam, what—"

He ignored her. "Tabby and I were talking over the break and she thinks only biological fathers make good dads. But I disagree."

"That's not what I said."

Again he ignored her. "So let's hear from you. What do you think? Adoptive fathers and stepfathers. Do they love their kids as much? Give us a call if someone raised you other than your biological father and you think that man did a good job. And if you're caller ten, we'll send you and your dad to the Salt Lick on Father's Day."

"Sam, this isn't our topic for today."

"Tabby, honey," he said in that voice he knew irritated her. "I know that. But you know how I like to flaunt convention."

"Okay, then. Dinner at the Salt Lick isn't even on our prize list."

He looked down at the desk in mock confusion as if looking for his notes. "Well, it should be. Stepfathers deserve to be appreciated, too. So I'll tell you what. Barbecue dinner at the Salt Lick will be on me."

Jeez, this was just like him. One minute she was confiding in him and the next he was telling the whole world about it.

"Sam, I think finding out the names of our listeners' pets is more interesting."

"Well, Tabby, the listeners disagree. We've already got some calls. Let's hear what Jessica from Roundrock has to say." He pushed the button to cue the caller.

"Hi, um..." the girl began slowly. "I've never called in before but I wanted to today because, Tabitha, I think you're wrong. My parents got divorced when I was just a baby and my stepdad raised me. When my mom died a couple years ago, he could have sent me to live with my grandma, but he didn't. He adopted me and now he's paying for me to go to college. I think he's really great, especially since I haven't heard from my real dad since I was two."

Sam nodded. Since the listeners couldn't see him, Tabitha could only assume he was nodding in satisfaction, a theory confirmed by the smug smile he shot her.

"Jessica, it sounds like you've got a really great stepdad," Sam said. "Thanks for calling in."

"I never meant stepfathers couldn't—" Tabitha began, but Sam cut her off before she finished her defense.

"Hold that thought. We've got another call. This time it's Roger. Roger, what do you think about this?"

"Frankly, Tabitha, I'm disappointed in you." The man spoke in a clear, confident voice. "I have three adopted kids and I love them every bit as much as I love the two my wife and I had naturally. It's the relationship that counts, not the genetics."

"Well, I agree, but—"

"No buts about it, young lady. Every child is precious. A miracle. For some people the journey to parenthood is longer than for others. That doesn't mean they enjoy it any less."

"Thanks for the call, Roger," Sam said smoothly, the picture of the genial radio deejay. The consummate performer. The snake! "Let's hear from the rest of you."

She silently banged her head against the heel of her hand as she watched the phone lines light up one after the other. All people calling to disagree with her.

Usually it worked the other way. He'd say something outrageous, she'd counter with logic and reason, and, with the exception of a few kooks, people called in to agree with her. How had he managed to maneuver her into being the bad guy?

She briefly considered the possibility he was merely trying to make his point about Bob, but she quickly dismissed it. Genuine concern just wasn't in him. He didn't want to have anything to do with this contest and was going to make her miserable the whole time it was going on. The pig.

TABITHA SMILED brightly at the man and his son approaching the station's table located near the starting line of the 5-K Run for AIDS Services of Austin. Jasmine, who wouldn't run five kilometers if there was a vat of ice cream waiting for her at the end of it, sat behind the table passing out bumper stickers and water bottles. The man took a water bottle, chatted with Jasmine for a minute, then, as he walked away, glared at Tabitha and said, "I'll have you know I'm a great stepfather!"

She felt the smile slip from her lips as she watched them disappear into the crowd of runners. When she glanced at Jasmine, she realized the other woman was suppressing a smile.

"This isn't funny," Tabitha snapped.

Jasmine gave up her attempts at subtlety and chuckled. "Yes, it is. What does that make? Six or seven so far this morning?"

"Eight." As she spoke, she held the corner of the table for balance, then reached back to grab her ankle, stretching her thigh. "Eight people have mentioned it so far. Of course, that's if you ignore the fifty-seven e-mails I got over the past two days, the thirty-something phone calls, and the twenty-two letters."

"Wow. Twenty-two letters?"

She turned around and repeated the procedure for the other leg. Looking over her shoulder at Jasmine, she explained, "An entire third-grade class wrote me about the importance of family. The teacher dropped them by the station on her way home."

"Not your typical fan mail, huh?"

"Not mine, no." She started in on her arms. "Sam may get stuff like this all the time. But not me."

She looked over her shoulder to where he stood by the towering live oak that shaded the parking lot. His back was toward the station table as he talked to a guy Tabitha had never seen before. She started to glance away, but the listener—she could only assume that's what he was since he seemed to be hanging on Sam's every word— was odd enough looking that she tilted her head to get a better view. He was tall and scrawny with a shock of red hair. Spindly legs stuck out from beneath cutoff sweats, which he'd topped with one of the appalling 'I ♥ Tabitha' shirts. He looked like an Irish Lyle Lovett.

Shaking her head in amazement, she turned her attention back to Jasmine. "Sam may be used to this kind of thing, but the listeners usually sympathize with me. I've never gotten hate mail before."

Jasmine pointed a crimson nail at her. "That's what you get for going on the air and saying stepfathers suck."

"I didn't say they suck."

"Humph. Close enough. You know *I* was raised by a stepdad."

"Not you, too. I'm going to kill Sam for this."

"What'd I do this time?"

She dropped her arms to her sides and turned to find Sam standing behind her. Luckily, Jasmine answered for her. "You made Tabitha look bad."

He shrugged, stepping around her as if dismissing her and her indignant irritation. "Is that all? Get over it."

"Get over it? What kind of advice is that? I got hate mail, Sam. Hate mail."

"I get hate mail all the time. It was just your turn. You'll get used to it."

"I don't want to get used to it. Besides, you provoked them." Jasmine opened her mouth as if she was going to say something, but before she could, Tabitha pointed her finger at Jasmine and snapped, "Don't you dare say *I* provoked them. I didn't. Sam took something I said completely out of context."

Jasmine held up her hands in surrender. "Whatever."

"Why would I have said that on the air?" she demanded. "I don't like to provoke people. That's Sam's job. I don't even like to attract attention."

Jasmine placed both palms hands down on the table and leaned forward and looked around at the crowd before stage whispering, "Then maybe you shouldn't throw a fit in the middle of the 5-K Run. You're scaring people."

She fumed for a second, sending both Jasmine and Sam vibes to back off before plastering a sweet smile on her face.

Okay, so she was stressed out. Obviously today wasn't going to go down in her personal annals as a shining moment of success. She'd have to muddle through it as best she could and then, as Sam had said, just get over it.

She turned to face the growing crowd, only to see the guy in the 'I ♥ Tabitha' T-shirt approaching her. Unease crawled across the back of her neck. She was not up to this today.

Shooting a look of annoyance at Jasmine, she muttered, "Just save me a juice bar at the end of the race, okay?"

She turned from the table to make her way to the starting line, hopeful she could blend into the crowd.

"Tabitha, wait up."

She heard Sam but didn't stop or even slow down. She ignored him until he caught up with her, then snapped, "What?"

"Where are you going?"

"To the starting line," she said deadpan. Obviously she wasn't the only one who wasn't operating on full steam.

"I thought you'd be working the table this year."

"Why would I be working the table? I always run." Well, okay, she admitted to herself, she never really ran the 5-K Run. Sam was usually right up in front, running the whole way. She was one of the stragglers, the people with good intentions but low energy who ended up walking the last four or so K.

Sam gestured vaguely in the direction of her belly and said, "Well...you know."

Holding up her hand, she interrupted him. "Never mind. I do know. I know exactly what you're going to say. And forget it. Just because I'm...*you know*, doesn't mean I'm going to stand around handing out doughnuts."

She turned and walked away. He followed, stopping her with a hand on her arm. He leaned in close. "But what I read in *Pregnancy for Dummies* said you should never start an exercise regime during pregnancy."

"*Pregnancy for Dummies*? That's appropriate." He didn't seem to appreciate her humor. "I'm not starting an exercise regime. It's only three miles. I walk almost that much shopping at—"

"Tabitha!"

The sound of Bob's voice stopped her short. Slowly she

turned on her heel and scanned the crowd. She saw him instantly. His Dockers and Oxford shirt stood out like a police road flare amid the wind shorts and jogging shoes. She watched him approach with a combination of dread and...and what?

Certainly not the pleasure she'd expected to feel.

For nearly a month he hadn't called, hadn't gone with her to the doctor's and certainly hadn't bought her Mooo Bars and Oreos. Yet, he showed up—here, of all places—and expected to talk to her. Obviously her plan to make him jealous was working. And sooner, much sooner, than she'd expected.

She struggled to muster up the satisfaction she knew she should feel at his easy capitulation, but when he finally reached her, all she could manage was forced enthusiasm.

"Bob!" she said, perhaps too brightly.

"Bob." Sam greeted him with all the warmth people usually reserve for a tooth extraction.

Bob looked her over, then before greeting her in any way turned to Sam. "We'd like a minute alone, if you wouldn't mind?"

"'We'?" Surprised by his presumption, she nearly told Sam to stay. But the anger written so clearly on Sam's face made her think twice. She nodded at him, then guided Bob carefully out of hearing range. "What do you want?"

"I'm worried about you, Tabby."

She cringed at the "endearment." Trying to keep her tone neutral, she reminded him, "I'm not yours to worry about."

He sighed and ran a hand through his hair.

While he fidgeted, she studied him with a sinking realization. He would never banish Sam from her thoughts.

Even when they'd been going out, he hadn't banished Sam from her fantasies. And that was back when she'd honestly thought Bob was the right kind of man for her. That was before he'd abandoned her and their child. Before she knew the truth about him.

Now that she knew what Bob was really like, she could never be with him again.

Regret, tinged with distaste, surged through her. She recoiled, taking a step back.

"That's why I came here today, Tabby. I wanted to talk to you about that."

Her heart started pounding—but with dread, not excitement. What would she do if he wanted to get back together with her?

"Okay..." She looked across the clearing to where Sam stood studying them.

"I know our breakup was sudden, but I think it was for the best. I'm sorry if it hurt you."

Relief washed over her, rinsing away her dread. She nearly laughed out loud. "Bob, I—"

"No, let me finish." He took in a shuddering breath, bolstering his courage. "We just weren't right together. I'll always respect you, Tabby. I just didn't think marriage was the answer."

Boy, was that ever the truth. Marriage to Bob was looking less appealing by the minute.

"I'll pay child support, of course. And—"

"You all right, Tabitha?"

She turned to see Sam looming behind her. With his arms crossed over his massive chest and the scowl lining his face, he looked like a disgruntled bouncer.

"I'm fine."

"You look upset." He nodded in Bob's direction. "Is he upsetting you?"

"I'm fine."

His gaze darted to Sam, then he shifted his stance, purposely excluding Sam. "I've discussed it with my parents, though. They were always fond of you." Again he glanced at Sam and again he tried to edge him out of the conversation physically. "They're prepared to set up a trust fund for the baby."

"Oh, that's very..." She hesitated, then felt Sam place a hand on her shoulder protectively. "That's very generous."

Bob nodded in satisfied agreement. "Naturally, they'll need to have the baby's paternity established."

Tabitha sucked in her breath as Bob's words hit her like a kick in the gut. Paternity? Bob's parents doubted the paternity of her child? Their lack of trust tore through her, weakening her. Instinctively she sagged against Sam, letting his strength support her.

"You bastard," Sam said. She felt the anger radiate off him, the tension in his muscles.

Bob balked. "It's a reasonable request. You can't expect them to just take your word for it that it's their grandchild."

"They wouldn't have to take my word for it. They could take yours." She no longer had the strength to deal with him.

Bob stepped toward her, hand outstretched. Sam cut him off.

"You should leave. Now." Sam bit off each of the words, making them a threat.

Bob either didn't hear it or chose not to listen. He edged back, but looked around Sam to catch her eye. "We still need to talk."

"Just go," she said again.

"This is just as hard on me as it is on you," he protested. "Maybe harder."

Before she could stop Sam, he hauled back and punched Bob.

Tabitha watched it all as if in slow motion—Bob's head popping back, the astonished expression on his face as he staggered back a step and then another and another before finally, hand raised to his face, he fell back and landed on the pavement.

She turned to gape at Sam. He stood there, a grim expression on his face, shaking the sting from his knuckles.

She should be mad at him—after all, he'd just punched her boyfriend, well, her ex anyway. But she *wasn't* mad. Maybe it was because she'd never had anyone step in to defend her like that. Maybe the right-wing conservatives knew what they were talking about and too many years of watching violence on TV had warped her brain. Or maybe it was just those damn pregnancy hormones. Whatever the cause, she wasn't angry and, worse still, she'd never thought Sam looked...yummier.

Oh, get a grip, Tabitha. You're a pacifist! This is no time to develop an adrenaline habit.

She tore her gaze from Sam—that alone was much harder than it should have been—and dropped to her knees beside Bob. "Are you okay?"

Bob glared at her. "No, I'm not okay!" A congested tone muffled his voice making him sound like a petulant child instead of a furious man. "I think he broke my nose!"

Bob moved his hand away from his nose to reveal a thin stream of blood pooling in his palm. It wasn't a lot of blood, certainly not enough to warrant his indignant sputtering, but it was enough to chase away that silly sexual zing she'd felt seeing Sam punch him in her defense.

"Oh, no," she cooed, hamming up her sympathetic concern to hide her true feelings. "Here, let me help." She raised the edge of her shirt to blot at the blood above his lip.

"He ruined this shirt!"

Tabitha watched in queasy disgust as Bob wiped his hand on her T-shirt rather than his own Oxford. Thank goodness someone from the crowd handed him a towel before he had a chance to lean over and blow his nose on her hem.

"It's just blood," she murmured, pressing the terry cloth gently to his face. He shied away from the pressure.

"Just blood? I could sue." He looked up to where Sam still stood over them. "I should sue!"

"Fine, buddy, you do that."

"I'm calling my lawyer right now." With his clean hand, he patted his pockets, looking for his phone.

"You don't have a lawyer," she reminded him.

"I could have a lawyer."

She met Sam's eyes. He stood there, so still, his arms hanging by his sides. But his fists were clenched, as if contemplating punching Bob again. "Don't worry," she said. "He doesn't have a lawyer."

"Let him get lawyer. I'd love to take this to court." His gaze shifted to Bob. "Let's hash this thing out in public. I don't mind who knows why I punched you. But what about you, Bob? What would your parents feel about that?"

Bob went pale beneath his red-faced fury. Tabitha glanced around, for the first time noticing the substantial crowd that had formed around them. Most people simply stared at them with blatant curiosity. But then she heard her name whispered and watched as understanding spread through the crowd. Seconds later, she heard the words "the boyfriend."

Bob looked at her, then at Sam, then at the dense ring of people, and finally back at her. "I'm sorry, Tabitha. I didn't mean for this to happen."

She felt her annoyance with his squeamishness melt a little. She sighed, helping him to his feet. "I know."

"Not gonna call that lawyer, after all?" Sam jeered.

Bob pointedly turned his back to Sam and said to her, "I want to talk about this. But not here." He paused to glare threateningly at Sam. "I have to go. But I'll call you later."

Hands on her hips, shaking her head in exasperation, she watched him stumble away. He certainly knew how to use an injury to its best advantage. Anyone who hadn't seen the actual punch would think a gang of motorcycle thugs had pounded him to within an inch of his life.

He said he'd call, but she wasn't sure she wanted to hear what he had to say. She glanced at Sam.

He frowned, crossed his arms over his chest and said, "You're going to yell at me for hitting him, aren't you?"

She stared at him for a long, silent minute. She *should* yell at him. It would serve him right. Instead she merely asked, "Why'd you do it?"

His frown deepened. "The guy's a jerk."

"So is Marty, and you don't punch him."

"What? I was supposed to stand here and listen to him talk to you that way?" Sam turned to study her. "Are you going to do it?"

"What? The paternity test?"

He nodded.

She considered her answer for a minute. "No. I don't believe I will. Either they'll believe me or they won't. Either they'll want to be involved with their grandchild or they won't. Either way, I don't want their money. I'll get by without it."

If Bob's actions today proved anything, it proved that she'd have to do this alone.

Her own actions proved something else entirely. All her talk of not being attracted to Sam was a load of bull. When it came down to it, she was as full of crap as Bob was.

7

"WHAT THE HELL happened out there?"

Newt looked up from his laptop. "Hey, Sam." He punched a couple of buttons on his laptop, then closed it and set it aside. He peered out into the yard beyond the porch on which he sat. "Out where?"

"At the 5-K. What the hell happened there?"

Newt frowned for a second, then said, "People came and ran five kilometers to raise money for AIDS research, I think."

"Don't be a smart-ass." He didn't have time for this. First, he'd spent Friday with a perpetual hard-on. Then he'd made an absolute ass out of himself today at the 5-K Run. If Tabitha stayed single much longer, he couldn't be held responsible for his actions.

Rubbing his forehead, he asked, "You were supposed to talk to Tabitha, remember?"

"Oh, yeah. That."

"So, what happened?"

"Well..." Newt took a long drink as if fortifying himself, "I decided not to do it."

Sam clenched his teeth, then forced through them a single word. "Why?"

"She looked kinda mad." Newt nodded slowly, clearly thinking it through. "It made me nervous. You know I don't do well with women in person."

"You didn't have any reason to be nervous. I told you

exactly what to say to her. Word for word. All you had to do was follow the script."

Newt shrugged. "I practiced saying it to myself, but I sounded kinda stupid."

The pure dejection on his face almost made Sam feel sorry for the guy. Almost. Newt had a job to do, damn it, and if he didn't pull it off, Sam would end up doing something stupid. Like kissing Tabitha. Or worse.

"Trust me. Tabitha won't think it's stupid."

"I got to meet Jasmine, though. She's nice."

"Yeah, Jas is great." Sam paced the length of the porch, then spun around and paced back. "We need to find some other place you can meet Tabitha."

"Jasmine gave me her e-mail address. Cool, huh?"

"Sure. Let's see... What are you doing next Wednesday? Tabitha's doing a remote in the afternoon at that new Mexican restaurant down south. Maybe that would work."

"Do you think I should e-mail her?"

"E-mail Tabitha? That's a great idea."

"No, I meant e-mail Jasmine."

"Why would you e-mail Jasmine?"

"'Cause I have her address. I don't have Tabitha's."

"I've got it." Sam crossed back to Newt's side of the porch and lowered himself to the other chair. He picked up Newt's laptop. "Do you have Internet access on this thing or should we use the computer inside?"

"I've a got a wireless system. I can get online anywhere within a hundred feet of the base station in my living room."

Sam studied him. He didn't sound enthusiastic. Must be nerves.

"Don't worry," he reassured him. "I'll be right beside you. We'll write the e-mail together."

A few minutes later they were online. Sam decided they should use her work e-mail since only a handful of people had her private e-mail address.

"Hey, she's online now," Newt said as they hovered over his laptop. "Do you want to send her an instant message? It'll be just like talking to her in person."

Sam nodded. "Perfect. You'll be able to tell her all the things you wanted to say today but didn't have the courage to."

TABITHA WAS JUST ABOUT ready to shut down her computer and go to bed when the instant message came through. She warily eyed the pop-up window with its message, "Want to talk?"

After spending the better part of the day at the 5-K Run and the rest of it online responding to the angry notes in her burgeoning In box, she wasn't sure if she was up to "talking" with anyone else online, especially since she didn't recognize the e-mail address.

But if she could convince just one more person that she didn't think stepfathers "sucked," she had to give it a shot. So, cautiously, she typed "Sure."

After a moment another sentence appeared. "I was sorry I didn't get to meet you when I came by to pick up my T-shirt."

Oh great. Another 'I ♥ Tabitha' guy. Just her luck.

Her fingers hesitated over the keyboard, then she typed. "So, you wrote one of the winning letters. Congratulations." She paused for a long moment, then added, "Who are you?"

There was an even longer pause from the mystery "I ♥ Tabitha" guy and she started to wonder if she'd scared him off.

Finally he wrote, "Newton Doyle."

Her breath caught in her chest at the sight of his name. She jerked her fingers away from the keyboard and clenched her hands into fists. She even scooted her chair back from her computer desk, eyeing the monitor cautiously.

Somewhere out there in cyberspace was the man whose letter had made her heart pound. The man who'd written the words her mouth had gone dry reading out loud. The man she'd avoided meeting.

The day he'd scheduled to come by and pick up his 'I ♥ Tabitha' T-shirt, she'd taken the coward's way out. She'd chosen not to risk destroying the illusion she'd created in her mind. But what would she do today?

After taking a deep breath, she lowered her hands to the keyboard, ignored the tremble in her fingers, and typed, "Hi, Newton. I remember your letter."

"I thought I'd lost you there for a minute. Where'd you go?"

She mentally tossed around a few fibs, but in the end answered truthfully. "Just trying to decide if I wanted to talk to you."

"I was at the 5-K today. I wanted to meet you but didn't have the courage to come up and talk to you."

She frowned, considering his words. "Why not?"

Instead of answering her question, he wrote, "Ignore that. It makes me sound like a stalker. I'm not."

Something in his tone—if you could call it that—made her smile as she typed, "Are you sure?"

"Yes. I don't want you to be afraid of me."

"Maybe I should be. After all, a girl can't be too careful." She sat back in her chair, waiting for his reply, surprised by the flirtatious tone of her responses.

"Yes, you can be too careful. Often, you are. You worry

too much. But I admire your caution. It makes you strong."

She frowned and reread his response. "Do I know you?"

"Define 'know.'"

Hmm. So he was going to be a smart-ass. It would serve him right if she didn't respond. But she did. "Have we met?"

"Yes."

"More than once?"

"Yes."

"Through work or socially?"

There was a long pause. Clearly he was trying to decide exactly what to say. Finally he typed, "Why didn't you want to read my letter on the air?"

"What? How did you know?"

"Unless U.S. mail is a lot slower than I thought, you waited over a week before reading it."

Oh, that. "I've gotten a lot of letters. It just took me a while to get to yours."

"And there was something in your voice when you read it out loud. It sounded like you didn't want to be reading it."

Hmm. Funny and sensitive. "You're right. I didn't want to read it on the air."

"Why not?"

She exhaled slowly. Just how honest was she willing to be with this stranger? But even as she asked herself that question, she typed. With the instant messaging, it felt less like talking to a stranger and more like talking to an old friend.

"I liked your letter. I didn't want to share it, I guess." She almost left it at that, then just before sending, added, "I didn't like that you'd written the letter just to win a stupid T-shirt."

"I didn't send the letter to win a T-shirt. I wanted to meet you."

Oh. "I thought you said you'd met me before."

"I had. But I wanted a date."

"Why not ask me yourself?"

"It's complicated."

Great. He was married. Or twelve.

The bottom dropped out of her stomach at the thought.

Again she scooted her chair away from the computer. Not wanting to answer at all, she grabbed her water glass and went to fill it up.

When she came back, he'd added, "I'm not married, if that's what you're thinking."

Hmm. Clever man. Or boy. "How old are you?"

"Old enough that you don't have to worry about breaking the law. Young enough to be attracted to you without being a lech."

His response made her smile. "Thank you. Very helpful."

"Tell me, Tabitha, do you dance?"

"Why do you want to know?"

"Just curious. You have the body of a dancer. Lean and graceful. Delicate and feminine. You make even the most mundane acts seem like ballet, sipping your coffee, reaching out to shake someone's hand, stretching your back after hours spent in front of a microphone."

She shivered as she read his words and a slow heat began to snake through her body. Rereading the words, she swallowed hard. "So you do know me through work."

"You're avoiding the question."

She laughed out loud at his sheer gall. "I'm avoiding the question?"

"Sure. You never told me whether or not you dance."

A smile flirted at her lips as she typed. She tried to wipe it from her face, but was having too much fun. "I took ballet for a couple of years. Paid for them myself with baby-sitting money. But I got into it too late."

Her typing slowed as she thought of all the years she'd yearned to take classes, but hadn't been able to afford them. She'd been heartbroken to learn she was too old to be taken seriously as a dancer.

"But you still have the grace of a ballet dancer. Ballet can be passionate, but restrained. Emotional, but structured. Rhythmic and wild, but with form. Joy, happiness, and eroticism under a thin layer of control."

Her breath came in short bursts as the room seemed to spin around her. She felt as dizzy as if he'd led her in a wild dance around the room.

She wasn't used to men saying things like this to her and didn't know how to respond. Certainly not to a stranger. So she did nothing.

After a minute he answered for her. "Yeah, you're definitely a ballet kind of girl."

Finally she found the courage to type, "If this is your way of asking me to go to the ballet with you, the answer is no."

"I don't like ballet."

She frowned. Instead of answering, she typed, "????"

When he answered, his words weren't what she expected. "I'm a two-stepper myself. Nothing beats a lazy dance across an old brick floor. Nothing beats the gentle sway of three-quarter time. The excuse to pull the woman you love into your arms and hold her close."

His answer left her with even more questions. First and foremost, was there some woman he loved that he two-stepped with? If there was, then why was he online chatting with her at ten o'clock on a Saturday?

After a moment when she still hadn't responded, he typed, "So what do you say, Tabitha? Could a ballet girl like yourself ever give a two-stepping guy like me a chance?"

Okay, that was definitely a come-on.

She pulled back from the computer, picked up her water glass and emptied it. She poised her fingers over her keyboard. Finally she typed, "I'm not sure that's a good idea."

The problem was, it sounded like a very good idea. Dangerously good.

Before she could add anything else, he replied, "Well, I'll be here, waiting. Let me know if you change your mind."

Before he could tempt her with anything else, she shut down her computer.

As she paced around her house, too restless to sleep, she admitted just how tempted she'd been. But her life was complicated now. After her disastrous meeting with Bob today, she wasn't sure what she wanted.

Not Bob, that was for sure.

The aching restlessness in her body made her yearn for a man who could get her juices flowing. Weaken her knees. Steal her breath. Someone who would make her feel all the wonderful tingling sensations she'd passed up in her relationship with boring, staid Bob. Truth be told, her body ached for Sam.

She didn't doubt, not for a minute, he'd haul her off to bed and coax sensations from her body that she'd only read about. And dreamed about in her wildest fantasies.

The restlessness in her heart yearned for even more, for someone like Newton. His lure had been strong enough when he was no more than a name on paper. Now that she'd talked to him online, she felt his pull even stronger. He had a depth and sensitivity Sam lacked. Yes, there was a sexual undercurrent in their conversation, but the emotional intimacy was even more dangerous.

She didn't know what scared her more. The fact that today she finally accepted she'd be having this baby alone. Or the fact that she was attracted to two very different men. And neither was the father of her child.

8

"DINNER AND A MOVIE." Tabitha, sitting cross-legged on her living-room floor, held up one of the contest entries as an example before dropping in onto the pile by her knee. "Dinner and a play." She gestured to a different pile. "Dinner and live music."

Sam picked his way across the floor as if each stack of papers was a land mine. He didn't want to tamper with whatever elaborate organizational scheme she had going.

It wasn't until he almost reached her that she looked up at him again. She nodded toward the pan he carried. "What's that?"

"Dinner."

She blinked in surprise. Then a hint of a smile crept across her face. "You brought me dinner?"

Something in his chest swelled at the sight of her smile. She didn't smile enough these days. He couldn't really blame her. Pregnant and alone, dumped by an asshole like Bob, what did she have to smile about?

"Thank you." Her smile broadened. "That's so sweet."

Sweet? She thought of him as sweet? That wasn't good.

When was the last time a woman had described him as sweet? Well, there was that redhead from about a year ago, but whipped cream had been involved, so that probably didn't count. Being "sweet" was about as bad as being a "really good friend" or having a "great sense of humor."

Of course, he couldn't let himself forget his position in her life. Co-worker, buddy, and all-around sweet guy.

He was here tonight to make sure things stayed that way. "Newt" would be writing her again, and by the end of the letter, he intended for her to be panting for a date with him.

All he had to do now was feed her lasagna and pump her for information. She'd be safely tucked away in a relationship with Newt before she knew what hit her. And Sam's relationship with her could get back on solid ground, just as he wanted.

Didn't he?

Before his battered psyche could come up with an answer, Tabitha rose from her seat on the floor.

"So, what'd you bring me?" she asked with a flirty little grin that went straight to his gut and sent his blood cells running for cover.

"Lasagna," he said, perhaps too harshly, as he fled for the sanctuary of the kitchen. "It'll need to be zapped."

Unfortunately she followed. He pretended to concentrate on her microwave controls, but looked up when she said, "My favorite. I can't believe you remembered."

"I didn't," he responded before realizing that in fact he had remembered. Panic shot through him, but he tried to dismiss it. So what if he knew she liked lasagna? Who didn't like lasagna? It certainly didn't mean anything he remembered that she liked lasagna. And mint-chocolate-chip ice cream. And daisies. Those were just the kinds of things they talked about on the show.

Besides, the lasagna hadn't even been his idea. He shoved the incriminating pan into the microwave oven and slammed the door shut. "Marie made it for you," he explained. "She watched *Moonstruck* last night. That always makes her wish she was part of a big Italian family."

"Oh, that's right. She made the best pot sticker dumplings after watching *The Joy Luck Club*. Well, thanks anyway. I appreciate it."

This time when she smiled at him, she was just Tabitha, not some mysterious temptress. Some of the tension seeped out of him. This was the Tabitha he could relax with.

After wrestling with her microwave, he followed her back to her living room. She faced the stacks of love letters, her shoulders hunched and head hanging in defeat.

Feeling an inexplicable need to comfort her, he rested his hand on her shoulder. To his surprise, she leaned against him, resting her back against his chest. The curve of her bottom pressed against his thigh.

His blood leaped in response to her nearness. He shifted slightly, praying she wouldn't notice the effect she had on him.

He told himself to step away from her, but he couldn't make himself do it. She seemed to need someone right now. He'd be damned if he let her down. He wasn't going to be another Bob. He'd grit his teeth and put up with it.

"Tell me about the letters you've looked at so far," he said.

"They're all the same. How am I supposed to pick? I was hoping at least one of them would be really wonderful."

A very unpleasant emotion—one he was afraid might be jealousy but didn't want to analyze too closely—ran through him. Fortunately, the timer rang, buying him time.

GET FREE BOOKS and a FREE GIFT
WHEN YOU PLAY THE...

Just scratch off the
silver box with a coin.
Then check below to see
the gifts you get!

SLOT MACHINE GAME!

YES! I have scratched off the silver box. Please send me the 2 free Harlequin Temptation® books and gift for which I qualify. I understand I am under no obligation to purchase any books, as explained on the back of this card.

342 HDL DRRP

142 HDL DRR5
(H-T-01/03)

FIRST NAME

LAST NAME

ADDRESS

APT.#

CITY

STATE/PROV.

ZIP/POSTAL CODE

7	7	7	**Worth TWO FREE BOOKS plus a BONUS Mystery Gift!**
🍒	🍒	🍒	**Worth TWO FREE BOOKS!**
♣	♣	♣	**Worth ONE FREE BOOK!**
🔔	🔔	🍒	**TRY AGAIN!**

Visit us online at
www.eHarlequin.com

DETACH AND MAIL CARD TODAY!

The Harlequin Reader Service® — Here's how it works:

Accepting your 2 free books and gift places you under no obligation to buy anything. You may keep the books and gift and return the shipping statement marked "cancel." If you do not cancel, about a month later we'll send you 4 additional books and bill you just $3.57 each in the U.S., or $4.24 each in Canada, plus 25¢ shipping & handling per book and applicable taxes if any.* That's the complete price and — compared to cover prices of $4.25 each in the U.S. and $4.99 each in Canada — it's quite a bargain! You may cancel at any time, but if you choose to continue, every month we'll send you 4 more books, which you may either purchase at the discount price or return to us and cancel your subscription.

*Terms and prices subject to change without notice. Sales tax applicable in N.Y. Canadian residents will be charged applicable provincial taxes and GST.

If offer card is missing write to: Harlequin Reader Service, 3010 Walden Ave., P.O. Box 1867, Buffalo NY 14240-1867

BUSINESS REPLY MAIL
FIRST-CLASS MAIL   PERMIT NO. 717-003   BUFFALO, NY

POSTAGE WILL BE PAID BY ADDRESSEE

HARLEQUIN READER SERVICE
3010 WALDEN AVE
PO BOX 1867
BUFFALO NY 14240-9952

NO POSTAGE
NECESSARY
IF MAILED
IN THE
UNITED STATES

When he came out a few minutes later with two plates of steaming lasagna, he found her once again seated on the floor shuffling through a stack of papers. She took her plate almost without looking up, shoveling a single bite into her mouth before setting it aside.

He lowered himself to the floor beside her before digging into his own food. "What exactly is it you're looking for in this perfect letter?"

She frowned in the direction of the obviously sub-par contest entries, shaking her head. "I don't know. I honestly don't. I guess I thought something would jump out at me."

In her heart she'd been waiting for that letter, the one that wouldn't fit into any of her perfectly chosen categories. And she had received such a letter. Newton's.

But when faced with the opportunity to meet him, twice now she'd refused. The first time, when he'd come by the station to pick up his T-shirt, she'd made a point of not being there. That she could excuse. After all, he'd still been a stranger. But after they'd chatted online, when he'd asked to meet her, she hadn't even given him an answer. What a coward she'd turned out to be.

With a determined shake of her head she returned her attention to Sam, who was watching her with a confused expression. She couldn't blame him. She was a little confused herself. But wasn't that the prerogative of pregnant women?

"Look, it's obvious now that I've seen them all that none of them is perfect."

"You've still got a couple of days."

Sam was at least pretending to understand, regardless of whether or not he actually did. Which was sweet of him. And surprising, since she wasn't used to Sam doing sweet things for her.

He picked up the stack nearest his leg. If she remembered right, it was the stack labeled "Yuck!" He quickly
flipped through the few entries that had made it into that
pile.

She glared at him when he chuckled.

"Okay, so none of these," he said. "What does that
leave?"

"A lot."

Sam frowned, thought about it for a minute, then
smiled. "I've got it." He waved a hand to indicate the remaining eight stacks of paper. "All of these were okay,
right? Just not great."

"Right."

"Okay." To her surprise, he reached out an arm and
swept up all the stacks within reach. He pointed to the
few stacks that he couldn't reach but she could. "Hand
me those."

She was a little reluctant to undo all her hard work
sorting the entries, but her system had gotten them nowhere. She might as well scrap it all and give his strategy
a shot.

Following his lead, she gathered the remaining entries
and began tapping the edges to square off the stack. Sam
reached out and grabbed the papers while it was still an
amorphous muddle.

"Trust me. That won't be necessary." He flashed her a
mischievous grin.

Then he tossed the papers in the air. "Catch one!"

For a flicker of a second, she sat stone-still as papers
flew and fluttered through the air like enormous snow-
flakes. Then, with a shocked laugh, she grabbed a page as
it floated past her. Triumphantly she held up her prize.

"Here it is. The most romantic letter. It just jumped out
at me," she joked.

"So who's the lucky guy?"

She looked down at the bottom of the page first, for his signature, then quickly scanned the letter. "Jim. He wants to take me on a moonlit cruise on Town Lake."

"This isn't the guy who sent a head shot, is it?"

She frowned, flipping the letter over to look at it front and back. "I don't know. I only brought the letters." Reading the page, she said, "It's for a local charity. Oh, and one of my favorite jazz bands will be playing."

"Sounds like the perfect first post-Bob date."

She stilled, then admitted, "Actually, it'll be my second post-Bob date." Now why did she feel so awkward admitting that?

"Really?"

Something in his voice caught her attention. She was surprised to see him frowning. Clearing her throat, she tucked a strand of hair behind her ear. "Chandi set me up on a blind date with her history professor."

"Another blind date?"

She nodded. "Next Wednesday. Jonathon Romone. He's English, apparently. Seems nice enough."

"You've met him?"

"Just talked to him on the phone." She forced a little enthusiasm into her voice. "He wants to go to a double feature at the Fellini film festival."

"Fellini? Sounds like an intellectual snob."

She nodded, cringing at the prospect of such a mind-numbing date. "Either that or he's one of those dark, brooding types."

Sam raised his eyebrow in speculation. "That would be better?"

She faked a shudder of disgust. "No! I can't stand men that get broody. If I wanted brooding I would reread *Wuthering Heights*. Heathcliff can pull it off, but frankly, these days, it just seems a little too codependent for my taste. If some guy is really that tortured, why doesn't he just get a therapist?"

"So don't go."

"No." Chandi and Jasmine were right, she needed the diversion. She needed something to take her mind off Sam. "He's probably a well-adjusted, happy-go-lucky fan of dark Italian films. Besides, it could be worse."

"How?"

"He could always be a rabid Jimmy Buffet fan. Besides, it's just one date. And if it's horrible—" she held up the winning letter "—I'll always have Jim as a backup."

As she carried Jim's letter to her desk, she ran a hand down her side to the small of her back where a steady ache had settled. She placed the paper on top, where she wouldn't lose it, and turned around.

She stretched first one arm and then the other over her head. "If I have to spend another minute sitting on the floor, hunched over a stack of papers, my back will never forgive me."

She continued stretching, relishing the relief it gave her muscles, until she noticed Sam staring at her. Unnerved by his dazed expression, she lowered her arms. "What?"

He swallowed, shoved a lock of hair off his face with one hand and pointed vaguely in her direction with the other. "Your, um, jeans are unbuttoned."

"Oh." Her hand jerked to the front panel of her jeans, where, as she well knew, the top two buttons of her five-button Levi's were undone. Flustered, she tugged at the hem of her shirt. She could feel a blush creeping up her neck and ruthlessly squashed her own embarrassment. It wasn't her fault that her favorite pair of jeans no longer fit. She was hardly overjoyed by it, but it was part and parcel of the whole maternity gig. "They're too tight," she explained. He still looked confused. "Because of the baby."

His eyes jerked up to meet hers then darted back to her stomach. A goofy, slightly awed grin tugged at his lips. Without looking away from her belly, he stepped closer. "The baby," he said almost to himself. His hand reached out, as if he might touch her, but then dropped. He shook his head slowly. "Damn," he murmured.

"Yeah, I know," she said. She felt her own smile spread across her face.

His reaction to the baby, so different than Bob's, warmed her. Bob's fear had only made her nervous and defensive. But this...this awe and wonder, which so closely matched her own emerging emotions, filled her with joy.

Wanting to share this miracle with him, she stepped closer, took his hand in both of hers and placed it on the gentle mound of her belly, which cradled the fragile life of her child.

To her surprise, he slipped his hand under the hem of her shirt. His fingertips, surprisingly rough, eased into the V made by her parted jeans and his thumb rested on her belly button.

Desire curled its way through her, replacing all the soft, gentle joy she felt about the life within her. How could this be Sam? How could his touch affect her this way? How could his fingers send shivers radiating through her whole body?

Suddenly she felt as if she couldn't breathe, as if all the air in the room had been replaced by some other inert element that her lungs couldn't process.

Did he feel it, too?

His gaze was focused on her belly. Her own eyes drifted closed and mentally she urged him to look at her face. And when she opened her eyes, she found him staring intently at her. He *did* feel it. He had to.

She took a long, shuddering breath, and then another, struggling to regain her control. Half hoping that she wouldn't. Praying that he'd lose his.

Slowly, he raised his left hand to the side of her face. He brushed his fingertips along her forehead and down her temple, tucking her hair behind her ear, then traced her jaw with his knuckles.

The feather-light caress made her burn from the inside out and made her mouth go dry. She swallowed, then moistened her lips.

Only when she heard his quick intake of breath did she realize how provocative that might look. He seemed to study her lips, so intently was he watching them. He was going to kiss her. She was so sure of it that she leaned into him, trapping his hand between them and brushing her nipples against his chest.

His left hand crept around her neck to urge her closer. Just before his lips touched hers, he murmured her name. "Tabby."

She felt the faintest stroke of his lips in the same instant that she heard that whispered word.

Tabby. He called me Tabby.

He never called her that. Unless they were on the air and he was trying to get a rise out of her. Was that what he was trying to do now? Get a rise out of her?

Well, he had.

She pulled back before the contact became anything more than a pale glimmer of a kiss. She pressed her lips together, blocking out the tingling heat.

She forced herself to step away from him. His brows pulled together, his eyes asking a question that his lips did not.

"This isn't a good idea." She hadn't wanted to say the words, knowing that, once said out loud, they would force them both to acknowledge what had almost happened. But she knew it had to be said. She could never pretend, even to herself, that the kiss hadn't happened. "It would be a mistake."

Sam's eyes narrowed and he stepped back, sliding his hands into his back pockets to keep from touching her again. If she wanted to ignore the power of that "mistake," that was fine by him. "Right," he snapped. "A mistake."

She wrapped her arms around herself as if she were cold, even though he was burning up. He thought he might have seen a tremble in her bottom lip, but he tore his eyes away from that particular temptation.

He turned toward the door, frustrated, still aching to explore her mouth, to drag her down to the floor and peel off her jeans. Oh, God, those jeans. Would he ever forget the sight of that narrow V of skin bared by those damn jeans of hers?

At the door he paused, his hand on the knob. He meant to leave. He had every intention of walking out her door and storming off.

And he probably would have, if only he hadn't looked at her one last time. All it took was a single glance over his shoulder and before he knew it, he was striding back across the room.

He stopped mere inches from her, then studied her for a second, noticing her mouth, parted in surprise, her brow, furrowed in confusion, and the look in her eyes, vulnerable and...and wanting.

A stronger man might have been able to resist that look. He might have been able to resist, if he hadn't in-

haled deeply. But when her sweet, feminine scent hit
him, he knew he had to taste her.

"I just need to..." Instead of wasting the time to finish
the sentence, he pulled her into his arms and covered her
mouth with his own.

Her lips were soft and full beneath his. Like heaven itself. She tasted sweet and heady. Like sin.

He held her tightly, leaving her no room to pull away.
This time, retreat would be harder. He wouldn't even let
her breathe until he'd kissed the hell out of her.

He'd only wanted to taste her, but now he couldn't
stop. He kissed her again and again. Not letting up until
he felt her kissing him back, her tongue sliding over his
and slipping into his mouth.

Her fingers burrowed in his hair, holding his head
close to hers while she deepened the kiss.

But then she abruptly pushed him away. Looking up at
him, her lips trembling but her eyes firm with conviction,
she said, "This is a mistake."

He nodded. "Absolutely."

Her fingers loosened then tightened convulsively. She
plastered her body against his and pulled his head back
down to hers. Her body pressed so close to his that he felt
her every curve. Every scrap of cloth that separated
them. Every button, every seam. Oh, those jeans. He
wanted to tear them off to reveal the tantalizing skin that
lay beneath.

He abandoned her lips to trail kisses across her jaw and
down her neck. He ached to yank off the cotton knit of her
T-shirt and expose her breasts, but didn't want to rush her,
didn't want to scare her into pulling away. He forced himself to slow down and concentrate on her neck, tracing the
path from her earlobe to her mouth and back again. But no

matter how slowly he forced his mouth to move, he couldn't seem to control his hands. They crept up under the hem of her blouse, paused only for a second on her rib cage, and then claimed her breasts.

As the weight of her breasts slid into his palms, two low moans tore through the room, hers and his own. Her moan subsided to a soft gasping breath as her head dropped back, her neck, her whole body arching toward him.

For a moment he simply held her, content to explore her breasts through the whisper-soft fabric of her bra. He learned the feel of her, finding the peaks of her nipples and running his thumbs across the sensitive, silk-clad skin. When he felt her hands clutching at his shoulders and heard her whimpered sigh, he knew touching her through fabric would never be enough. He had to see her.

His desperate fingers fumbled for the clasp, but he couldn't release the damn thing. Frustrated, he yanked her T-shirt up and over her head and let it drop unnoticed onto the floor. He battled the stubborn clasp for only a moment longer before simply shoving her bra down to free her breasts. She struggled with the straps before freeing her arms, but he hardly noticed. All he could think was that Newt had been right. She really did have great tits. Perfect. Knock-him-to-his-knees perfect.

Pale and smallish, almost frail-looking, they were firm with nipples the color of her cheeks when she blushed. His mouth went dry just looking at her. She was a boyhood fantasy come to life. Her nipples were hard and puckered, begging to be tasted. He leaned down and traced one perfect peak with his tongue. A shudder followed in the wake of his tongue. Then, as he took her nip-

ple into his mouth, she went wild in his arms, tearing at
his shirt, clutching at his skin, and coming apart completely.

He'd never seen or felt anything like her response. He
licked and lapped, nibbled and suckled, all the while
driving her closer to her release and fighting his own
urge to possess her completely.

He could hardly stand having her this hot and willing,
yet not be inside of her. He needed her now, before she
climaxed and came to her senses. He urged her toward
the sofa with tiny baby steps. He eased her back, lower-
ing her to the waiting cushions.

"No," she gasped.

He stopped, heart pounding, and lifted his head to
look at her.

She shook her head. "Not the sofa. The wall."

It took him a second to realize what she meant. Then
relief flooded him. She was still his.

He backed her up two short steps, braced his left arm
behind her to protect her bare shoulders and pressed her
to the wall. He redoubled his attention to her breasts,
pausing only when her hands wiggled between them to
tug his shirt over his head. Then her fingers attacked the
closure of his jeans.

She had already loosened her own jeans and was shoving them down her hips before he realized what she intended. He stopped and rested his forehead against her
shoulder. The thundering of her heart matched his rag-
ged breathing.

This was Tabitha. His Tabitha. He wanted her as he'd
never wanted anything. But this was wrong. The first
time shouldn't be a quickie up against a wall. Their first
time should be on a bed, with her laid out in front of him,

where he could spend hours exploring her body, ravishing her. Driving her wild.

She threaded her fingers through his hair and nudged his head up. She wrapped an arm around his shoulders, a leg around his hips and brought her mouth to his. His free hand instinctively reached for her leg and found bare flesh. He couldn't resist sliding his hand up the length of her leg and under the elastic of her panties. He found her wetter, hotter, slicker than he'd ever dreamed.

As if that wasn't heaven enough, she tugged his jeans and underwear low on his hips and slipped her hand between them to grasp his erection. Her thumb ran over the tip and her fingers, damp with sweat and need, massaged the shaft, nearly sending him over the edge.

Still, he raised his head and rasped, "Are you sure?"

"Oh, yes."

He kissed her again, cradling her body against his while he gave her time to change her mind if she was going to. But he wasn't gentleman enough to ask again.

She lifted her head and asked, "Condom?"

He nodded. "In my wallet. Back pocket."

It took only seconds for her to empty his wallet, find the condom and toss the remains on the floor. A few more for her to tear open the package and ease the latex down his length. And by the time she was done, he still hadn't figured out how to get her panties off. So he simply shoved the fabric aside and eased inside of her.

She arched against him, taking all of him in one smooth motion. He wanted to slow down, but couldn't, not with her gasping out her pleasure, pushing him closer and closer to the edge.

She clasped his head to her breast. He pulled her nipple into his mouth and matched the suckling of her nipple with the rhythm of his thrusts. In seconds she reached her climax and milked his own from deep within him.

As the last tendrils of release shuddered through him, he knew one thing. All the Bobs and Newts and Jonathons of the world could go to hell.

Tabitha was his.

9

SAM HAD GREAT CREDIT.

In her earlier haste to retrieve the condom from his wallet, she'd scattered his credit cards on the floor and now they lay there still, little platinum reminders of her own insatiability. She buried her burning cheeks against the crook of his neck, trying to keep from squirming in shame.

Sam, now seated on her sofa, his legs spread out across its length, held her on his lap. One arm supported her shoulder, the other gently stroked her hair. Fifteen minutes had passed since they'd made love against the wall. Fifteen minutes during which Sam had carefully pulled away from her, covered her with his T-shirt when her own wasn't easily within reach, and settled onto the sofa with her on his lap. Fifteen minutes that felt like a lifetime.

It had never occurred to her that the kind of man who would make love to a woman up against her living room wall, after driving her to near orgasm by merely kissing her breasts, would also be the kind of man with a good credit rating.

The absurdity of that thought struck her immediately. Yet she couldn't get it out of her head. Her one remaining functional brain cell—the rest must have been completely fried during the combustion—told her she was only obsessing about Sam's credit because it kept her from thinking about all the things she didn't want to think about right now.

Guilt and anxiety mixed in equal parts in her belly like one of Chandi's killer martinis, making her feel about as sick as she had the time she'd tried one.

Dear God, what had she done?

What had she been thinking? Sex with Sam? Up against a wall? In her living room? In front of her picture window?

She had neighbors, for goodness' sake!

In her mind flashed an image of the elderly couple from down the block, the Hansens, out taking their nightly walk, happening by her house. Poor Mr. Hansen had a weak heart. She'd probably killed him!

Okay, Tabitha. Calm down, she told herself. Mr. Hansen was probably safely at home watching the evening news. If he'd had a heart attack Mrs. Hansen would be banging down the door. Probably no one saw them having sex. If anyone had...well, she couldn't do anything about that. She had to concentrate on the problems she could do something about. She had to get herself back under control.

She had to get off Sam's lap.

SAM KNEW the very instant Tabitha started thinking again. She'd been snuggled against his chest, lush bare legs pulled in close to her body, one hand tucked under her chin, the other resting against his heartbeat. She'd been so contented he would have wondered whether or not she was even awake if it hadn't been for the occasional flutter of her eyelashes.

He felt awareness return to her, not slowly, as it had

for him, but in short, rapid bursts. The knowledge of what they'd done hit her as quickly as the passion had. He felt it in her tensing muscles, her quick intake of breath and her heart beating so fast he felt it pound against her ribs.

If it had been any other woman curled up naked on his lap, he'd be trying to figure out how to get her off of him so he could dash for the door. But tonight, with Tabitha, that wasn't what he wanted. He wanted…to hold her.

To hold her? Where had that come from? What was wrong with him?

Get a grip, Sam, he told himself. *This is Tabitha. It'll be okay. You'll figure it out.* And it wouldn't kill him to keep holding her on his lap while he did. In his arms, she felt frail and delicate. And she smelled good. Sweet, like vanilla.

He let his arms tighten around her and felt her wiggle against him in response. Not a cute little seductive wiggle. He would have enjoyed that. Not a snuggle-in-deeper wiggle, either. An agitated I-want-down wiggle.

He tightened his arms around her, unsure what to do, but when she wiggled again, he forced himself to loosen his arms. She swung her legs to the floor and slipped awkwardly off his lap.

"Where are you going?"

Without meeting his eyes, she gestured vaguely toward the bathroom. She walked backward in that direction, seemingly unaware of the papers her shuffling feet scattered across the floor. Then, a few feet from the hallway, she turned and dashed for safety, giving him only a glimpse of her pale, perfect behind before she disappeared.

He heard the click of a door closing somewhere in the house. He leaned forward, rubbing the heels of his hands over his forehead and waited. He didn't know how long he sat there, alone on her sofa, elbows propped on his knees, forehead resting in his hands, waiting for her to come out of the bathroom. Minutes? Hours?

Long enough. He'd waited long enough. He stood, zipped his jeans, and went in search of her bathroom. He found it, the door open, the room empty. Through an open door at one end of the hall, he could see a desk and a large cardboard box neatly labeled Baby Linens. The door at the other end, which had to lead to her bedroom, was closed.

He approached the door cautiously, not sure what to expect. He raised his hand to knock, but instead flattened his palm against the wood and for a second just stood there. Silent. Listening for signs of life from the other side of the door, he heard none. Was she even in there? She had to be. Her house wasn't that big.

He knocked. "Tabitha?"

She didn't answer at first, but he heard a quick intake of breath through the door followed by a slight scuffle. "Um...I'll be out...in a minute."

She sounded out of breath. Or...upset.

His hand jerked away from the door and curled into a fist. Ah, crap. What had he done?

He paced about two steps down the hall before turning to stare at the door, willing it to open, hoping Tabitha would step out and walk straight into his arms.

The door didn't open. He started counting silently. When he reached fifty, he stepped forward, grabbed the knob and pushed. The door flew open...about five inches before slamming to a stop.

What the hell?

Then he looked down. Through the five-inch crack between the door and the doorjamb, he could see what looked like...a dresser shoved against the door.

For a moment he simply stared at the patch of dresser. His brain was still working at about half speed.

"Tabitha?" he called.

"Go away," she ordered through the door.

Then the dresser inched forward, toward him, easing the door closed, and suddenly his mind cleared. She was blocking her bedroom door with that dresser. She was trying to lock him out.

Cursing his sluggish mind, he shoved his foot in the door, hoping to block her progress while he figured out what the hell was going on. No answer immediately came to mind. "What the hell are you doing?"

The only answer was silence.

"Come on, Tabby. Open the door." The dresser crept forward enough to begin pinching his foot. "Okay, okay! Stop. My foot's in the door."

She said nothing, but she must have stopped pushing against the dresser because the pressure on his foot eased a bit. Encouraged, he wrapped his hand around the edge of the door, angling for a better view into the bedroom. Just beyond the dresser, he saw her bed. A simple mission-style bedframe, a plain white quilt. Just what he would have expected from her. Clearly this was her sanctuary from the world. Unfortunately, right now, it was her sanctuary from him, as well.

"You should come out. Hiding in there isn't going to solve anything."

"Can't we just forget this whole thing ever happened? It was a mistake. Just a terrible mistake."

That word—mistake—seemed to slice through him. For him, it had been amazing. The best sex he'd had in a long time. Maybe the best sex he'd ever had. Sex that shook him to his very soul.

And, for her, it'd been a mistake.

In his narrow view of her room he saw her sink onto the edge of her bed. In tiny increments she slumped forward. Elbows onto her vulnerable knees. Face to her palms. Hair fluttering forward, hiding his view of her face. "Go away."

"I'm not gonna go away. I'm not leaving you like this."

"Sam, please go away. I need…I need to be alone right now." Her voice broke as she spoke and the sound tore at his heart.

He squeezed his eyes closed and thumped his forehead against the door. Oh, God, what had he done?

All this time he'd been so pissed at Bob for dumping her, for hurting her, for making her cry. And now he'd hurt her, too.

He was a fool and a bastard. He never should have touched her. He knew there was chemistry between them. He'd known all along how great sex would be. He'd also known how vulnerable she was right now.

If she wanted to be left alone, then that was the least he could do.

He turned to leave. He made it halfway down the hall. But the sight of the box labeled Baby Linens stopped him in his tracks. Somehow, he'd forgotten about the baby. He'd just made love to a pregnant woman and been so caught up in the moment he'd forgotten she was pregnant.

On top of it all, he'd just let a pregnant woman move heavy furniture. And he'd been about to walk out on her, leaving her to move the furniture back all by herself. He was really on a roll tonight.

He spun on his heel and made his way back to her

room. He may have screwed up everything else, but he'd be damned if he wasn't going to move her dresser back before he left.

He found her still sitting on her bed, staring at a spot between her feet.

"Tabitha."

Her head jerked up in surprise.

"I thought you'd left."

"I can't leave you like this. I—"

She jumped to her feet and interrupted him. "Well, you're going have to."

"No—"

Before he got out any more of his protest, she crossed the few steps to the door and slammed it shut.

Well, maybe slam wasn't quite right, since it hadn't been open very wide, but, still, she used enough force to make herself feel a little better. But only a very tiny amount better.

She'd given up on moving the dresser those last few inches. Still, she wanted the door closed. So she hoisted herself onto the dresser top and sat cross-legged with her back against the door.

She leaned her head back, knocking it gently against the door and cursing herself. What kind of woman locked herself in her bedroom after sex? God, she was a coward.

A coward—and wimp, since moving her small dresser had left her panting. After the baby came, she'd have to start exercising. Not that her cardiovascular health was her first concern right now. She had bigger problems to worry about. Sam being at the top of the list.

"Tabby?"

She thought after two years she knew every tone of his voice, every timbre, every inflection, every pitch. But she'd never heard him sound like this. If she hadn't known better, she might have thought that what she heard in his voice was concern.

But this was Sam on the other side of the door. Mr. One-Night Stand himself. And she knew him well. If there was concern in his voice it was probably because he wasn't sure how to lock her front door on the way out.

Frankly she'd always felt sorry for those nameless women who threw themselves at him. And now she'd become one of them.

"Tabby, I just wanted to—"

"Look, Sam, I know. You want to talk. I heard you the first time. But I *don't* want to talk about it. I know what happened was totally out of character—for me, anyway—but I've been doing a lot of odd things. This must just be some weird hormonal glitch. There's no other explanation. This isn't the kind of thing I normally do. You know me. I'm responsible. I'm the person who keeps an extra twenty tucked into the back pocket of her purse for emergencies. I'm a member of AAA." There was no response from the other side of the door. She didn't need one. She was preaching now, pacing back and forth in front of the dresser.

"I'm not the kind of woman who would do this sort of thing. I don't have sex with men I don't care about. I never have. I never would. This has to be hormones. It's the only explanation that makes sense."

Suddenly aware of how silent he'd been during her tirade, she called, "Sam?" When there was no answer, she called out again, a little louder. Still nothing.

He'd left?

She walked over to the edge of her bed and sank down, waiting for the flood of relief. It didn't come.

She felt the prickling of tears behind her eyelids and

blinked rapidly. Despite her best efforts, the tears slipped free to trail down her cheeks. Slowly, she eased over onto her side, pulling her legs up to her chest with one hand and covering her eyes with the other.

She lay there, full of silent fear, turning it over and over again in her mind. What had she done? And why? Why had she done it?

Somehow, this one reckless act of passion shook her more than even an unplanned pregnancy. True, the baby and the responsibilities of motherhood were huge, almost insurmountable obstacles in her life. But that, at least, hadn't been her fault. She had done everything right. She'd been in a stable relationship. She'd been careful. She'd used birth control. She hadn't done anything wrong. As scary as being a single mother seemed, at least she couldn't blame herself.

But this…this was a whole other kettle of fish. She had no one to blame but herself.

How had this happened to her? How had her life gotten so off course? What was the point of doing everything right, of staying in control, of keeping everything together, if it could all suddenly fall apart?

Why did doing the wrong thing have to feel so good? And why, oh, why, couldn't she get the feel of him out of her mind? She could close her eyes and feel his hands on her body. And smell him, as if he was standing right behind her. Her eyes jerked opened, afraid that he'd somehow broken down the door.

He hadn't. But when she looked down, she saw that she was still wearing his shirt. No wonder she still smelled him.

Relieved that she wasn't going crazy, she grasped the hem of the shirt, ready to yank it off and toss it across the room when a flash of movement caught her attention. Instinctively, she crossed her arms over her chest. She studied the window near her bed, sure she'd seen movement outside. Still, she gasped when something banged against the window frame.

Sam. Through the glass, she could just make him out. What was he doing out there? And why was he banging on her window?

Her questions were answered two bangs later when she noticed that all his banging had rattled loose the latch on her window. From across the room, she watched it slip free. She lunged across the bed to escape out the door.

But she was too late. A hand, large and determined, reached over her shoulder to slam the door shut. Her eyes closed, defeat weighing them down. She could feel him behind her, looming over her. She sucked in a deep breath, searching for the courage that had abandoned her earlier. But within her, she found no courage, only the need to lean back against him and absorb some his strength.

She pried open her eyes and looked over her shoulder.

His expression was grim and determined as he shook his head. "Not again."

She turned around. He didn't step back, but kept her trapped, wedged into the corner made by the dresser, the bed, and his body. And, oh, lordy, what a body it was. Worn, low-slung jeans, zipped but not snapped, and a bare chest. Impossibly wide shoulders. How did a man who worked in radio get shoulders that wide? What did he do, move pianos in his spare time?

She leaned back as far as she could, but still mere inches separated them. She searched for something to say that might placate him, but could think of nothing. A lifetime of manipulating words, of talking herself out of and into situations, of using language to get what she wanted, and now they failed her completely.

Her only hope was to appeal to his more logical side. "Look, we both know that this was a mis—"

He cut her off before she could even finish the word. "Don't use that word again. Ever."

His order only increased her defensiveness. "Or what?"

His eyes narrowed even more and the muscles of his arm, which was still propped against the door behind her, tightened. Out of the corner of her eye, she had a clear view of that bicep. How was it she'd never before noticed how powerful his arms were?

She couldn't help remembering when that same arm had been braced on the wall behind her, cradling her head. The thought sent a shiver through her. Dear God, it had been unlike anything she'd ever experienced. It'd be so easy to close the distance between them, to pull his head down to hers and experience it all over again. They were inches from any number of vertical and horizontal surfaces that would serve.

Just when she thought he might ignore her challenge, he shook his head and said, "Just don't."

His expression, so serious, so sad, so unlike him, gave her pause. But before she could get reeled in again, she ducked under his arm and slipped free.

As if to ward him off, she held up a hand and tried to dissuade him. "Okay, you want to talk? I'll talk. But you stay right there. Away from me." He frowned and propped one hand on his hip. She firmly reminded herself that she should not be entranced by the way his chest muscles moved. "And for goodness' sake, put on a shirt."

"You're wearing my shirt."

She looked down at herself, blushing furiously. "Sorry."

"Look, Tabitha, if you don't want to talk. We won't talk. You want to be alone. I'll leave."

She narrowed her eyes in suspicion.

He held up his hands, palms facing her. "I just came back to move the dresser. It's too heavy for you."

Oh, God. She'd been right. He was being Mr. One-Night Stand. He really was leaving. He wanted to move furniture for her. This was the only thing worse than wanting to make sure he knew how to lock the door on the way out.

All of her fears and doubts about what had happened began to multiply. Like fertile little rabbits, they started popping up all over the place.

She sank to the edge of the bed and dropped her head into her hands. When that didn't calm her, she dropped her head to her knees.

"Come on, Tabitha. Everything is going to be okay."

She glared up at him. She knew when she was being placated and it only infuriated her more. "Okay? Everything is not going to be okay. Everything is very far from being okay! Maybe for you everything will be okay. But you're not pregnant. I am."

"Yeah, I know."

"But, Sam, I'm pregnant."

"Yeah. I know. I was there when you found out. I've been there all along. I thought we'd dealt with this issue."

"Dealt with it? No, I haven't dealt with it. Obviously I haven't dealt with it or this wouldn't have happened. This wasn't just hormones—it was also panic. I mean, obviously this whole thing was brought on by delayed shock."

"Delayed shock? What the hell is that suppose to mean?"

"Well, it must be, right? Because, otherwise, I never would have slept with someone like you."

"I'm going to forget you said that, because you're upset."

"Of course I'm upset. I've completely lost control of my life and I think we're both aware that our having sex isn't going to fix things."

Then it hit her. That's exactly what she'd been trying to do. Having sex with Sam was a desperate—possibly psychotic—attempt to regain control of her life.

Oh, no. Why hadn't she seen it before?

Try as she might, she hadn't been able to keep herself from wanting him. So, forcing the issue, ordering him to make love to her, to act out her fantasy of having sex with him up against her living room wall, was her way of taking control of her desires.

She dropped her head back into her hands as the horrible truth washed over her.

Even worse, her "plan" had backfired. Having sex with Sam hadn't given her control over her passion. It had only made her want him more. Yet, somehow, understanding what exactly she'd done, knowing why she'd done it, made her feel better. And gave her the strength to be sensible. "Sam, we'll just have to do what we can to put this behind us. To forget what happened here and go back to just being co-workers—"

"Damn it, Tabitha," he interrupted. "We're not just co-workers. There's been chemistry between us from the start. Neither of us did anything about it because the timing wasn't right, but now that Bob's out of the picture, we owe it to ourselves to see where this is going."

For a moment she could only stare at him in shocked

silence, his words churning in her mind. So it wasn't just her? The desire that had been gnawing at her for years wasn't hers alone. He'd felt it, too?

"Besides," he went on, "we're friends."

"Friends?" Every weekday morning for the past two years she'd been the butt of his jokes, played the straight man for him, and he thought they were friends? "We're not friends. We hardly know each other."

"Bullshit. I know you. I know you better than Bob knows you."

"Don't be ridiculous."

"Where's Bob now? If he knew you half as well as I do, he'd be here. If it'd been me instead of Bob, you wouldn't be in this situation, because I know how scared you are."

She wrapped her arms around her waist, hugging herself, disconcerted by his words and disappointed by them, as well. He hadn't said what she most needed to hear. That if it had been him instead of Bob, he never would have left her. Angry with herself for harboring such useless hopes, she said defensively. "That...that doesn't mean anything. It doesn't take a genius to figure out that I'm scared."

"Fine. But I do know you. I know you listen to oldies when you're at home. I know you like oatmeal cookies better than chocolate chip because you think they're some sort of cookie underdog. I know you don't like football because you say it's too violent, but you're a secret hockey fan. I know you vote in every election, even the minor ones. I know you always vote Republican. And I know that when you read the newspaper you save the comics for last so that you'll end on a good note. And if you don't know me at least that well, then you haven't been paying attention."

As he spoke, all her tumult hardened inside her. By the

time he was done, she knew just what to say to make him leave.

"You're right, Sam. I do know you. I know how much you value your independence. I know how you treat women. Going on a second date is your idea of a long-term relationship. Chemistry or not, friends or not, this thing between us is over before it even started. I'm pregnant. You may have forgotten that, but I haven't. I have this baby to think about. Even if I wanted to have a fling with you, I couldn't. In less than seven months I'm going to be a mother. I have to think about that. So unless you want to get married and be the father to my child for the next eighteen years of his or her life, I don't have time for a fling."

10

HER WORDS SLAMMED into him with the force of a three-hundred-pound linebacker. Marriage? Fatherhood? What the hell was she talking about?

As the silence stretched between them, he waited for her to say something that made sense. Anything.

Seconds stretched endlessly, each lasting an eternity.

He'd read about this kind of thing. How in moments of extreme trauma, the body's biological clock actually slows. As far as he knew, it happened when people were in car crashes and convenience store holdups. And, apparently, when a man heard the word "marriage."

The sensation of time screeching to a halt was accompanied by a catastrophic leap in his heart rate. He felt as if the floor had just evaporated, dropping him down the rabbit hole.

In truth, the rabbit hole had first gaped beneath him the second his fingertips had glided over the velvety-soft skin of Tabitha's belly.

The sight of her standing there in his T-shirt—his lucky T-shirt, no less—brought him back to square one. Just as he'd always suspected, delectable little Tabitha was a dynamo in the sack. Right now, it took every ounce of male fortitude not to haul her across the bed, yank that shirt off, and make love to her again.

All of which proved what he'd known all along. He was a Class-A bastard.

Here she was, crying, upset enough to throw out the word marriage—not that, after he got over the initial shock, he took her seriously—and all he could think about was sex.

"What? No comment? Here's something I never thought I'd see—you at a loss for words." She crossed her arms over her chest, glaring at him.

"What do you want me to say?" he asked.

Her lips curled with disdain. "Nothing. I don't want you to say anything at all. I want you to go."

He stared at her, looking past the sexy rumple of her hair, past the lush curves barely hidden beneath his shirt, past the kiss-swollen lips he'd never again be able to ignore, and saw the fragility she hid so well.

And behind that fragility, maybe he saw hope. But hope for what? Surely she wasn't serious about marriage.

Was she?

No, he reassured himself. *No, surely not.*

But...

No, it was ridiculous. She knew as well as anyone else that he wasn't the marrying the kind. She'd thrown out the word marriage just to scare him.

Not knowing what else to say, he shrugged, palms up in supplication, and said, "Tabitha, I'm sorry."

Then, in an instant, the illusion of frailty vanished. She raised her chin and glared at him from across the bed. "Get out of my house."

"I—"

"Go." She pointed to the door.

"But—"

"I mean it, Sam. I don't want to be anywhere near you right now."

It wasn't the words as much as the tone of her voice—anger tinged with disgust—that made him believe she meant it. He nodded stiffly, then crossed to her dresser. He shoved the damn thing out of his way.

He turned and looked at her one last time before leaving.

Okay, so he'd blown it. This time. For now, he'd retreat. He'd give her until Monday. By then, he'd have a plan.

What exactly that plan entailed, he had no idea. Not marriage, that was for sure, but something...else. After all, Marie was right. Why couldn't they just be together and not break up? That wouldn't be so hard, would it?

Surely he could devise a plan to make Tabitha see that. One that would make her forget all her ridiculous, antiquated ideas about marrying the father of her child or anyone else. One that would get her into his bed, where she belonged.

IT WAS AFTER NOON when Tabitha cracked open her front door, fully intending to shoot the person on the other side. She'd be doing society a favor. Anyone who would pound relentlessly on a door for ten minutes must be sublimating violent tendencies.

Peering through the narrow gape between door and door frame, she caught a glimpse of short bleached hair and inch-long, hot-pink nails. Jasmine. Darn it. She couldn't shoot her best friend.

Tabitha stepped back and allowed the door to swing open.

Jasmine raked a disdainful gaze down to Tabitha's floppy white socks then back up to her sleep-matted hair. "You look like hell."

"Thanks." She could just imagine. Not that she needed to hear it from Jasmine.

"What happened to you?"

"Don't ask." She winced, squeezing her eyes shut to block out the intrusive sunlight. The second her eyes closed, her imagination kicked in, flooding her with images of *him*.

Her eyes popped open, then narrowed into a glare. "Just come in and shut the door. All that sunshine is annoying." She padded toward the kitchen in search of caffeine. Yes, it was bad for the baby, but this was an emergency.

She dug the last of her caffeinated coffee grounds from the freezer, then asked, "What are you doing here?"

Jasmine's eyebrows shot up. "I can't believe it. You forgot?"

Tabitha glanced at Jasmine as she filled the pot with water. "If I'd remembered, would I have to ask?"

"Saturday? Noon? The little Thai restaurant by the mall? Lunch before hitting all the spring sales? Any of this ringing a bell?"

She tapped down a frustrated groan. "Now it is."

"So what's up?"

"I'm sorry. I had—" *Great sex? Multiple orgasms?* "—a rough night." She shrugged, hoping in vain that Jasmine would let it ride at that.

"Obviously. But how could you forget plans we made less than twenty-four hours ago?"

Oh, let's see, by risking my heart and having sex with Sam.

Tabitha paused, hand in midair as she reached for a coffee mug. Her heart? Where had that come from? She hadn't risked her heart by having sex with Sam, had she?

Preoccupied by that disturbing possibility, she handed Jasmine a cup without even looking at the other woman. The sound of the mug clattering to the counter yanked her attention back to the moment.

"Dang, girl. What's up with you?" Jasmine stood, hands propped on her hips, waiting for an answer.

"Huh?"

"You just handed me a coffee mug when I'm standing five feet away. And you know I don't drink coffee."

"Well, I..."

Before she could formulate any kind of defense, Jasmine crossed the room, cupped Tabitha's chin and tilted her face first one way then the next, studying her. Whatever Jasmine saw in Tabitha's expression made her eyes go wide with surprise.

"You got laid."

"What?" Tabitha squeaked before clearing her throat and trying again. "I mean, why would you think that?"

"You're glowing."

Tabitha jerked away. "Don't be ridiculous. I'm not glowing."

"You are."

"What? Five minutes ago, I looked like hell and now I'm glowing?"

"Five minutes ago I was distracted by the beginnings of a very bad hair day and your questionable taste in sleepwear. Now that I've had a chance to look past those things, I can see you're definitely glowing. And there are only two reasons why women glow."

She didn't want to ask. Unfortunately she didn't have to.

"Either she's just had great sex. Or she's pregnant."

Tabitha's heart leaped in her chest.

"And since we both know you're not pregnant, it's got to be great sex."

Her heart landed with a thump right on top of her stomach. As she fought back a wave of nausea, she tried to reassure herself. Her secret was safe—at least, one of them was.

Hiding her anxiety behind her coffee addiction, she jerked the pot out from beneath the drip spout then slid her mug in its place to collect enough for at least one fortifying gulp. She listened with half an ear while Jasmine babbled on about how—according to *Cosmo*—sex, particularly great sex, increased blood flow to the delicate skin on a woman's cheeks.

Tabitha wasn't fooled. Jasmine was just trying to lower her defenses before segueing into a serious interrogation about who exactly was responsible for the glow. Jasmine would want details, and Tabitha wasn't about to spill these particular beans. She'd have to lie.

She replaced the pot, then took a sip of the still-scalding coffee. Who could she pin this on? Bob? No, a year and half and he'd never caused so much as a glimmer, let alone a glow. She just couldn't lump him in the same category as Sam.

And that was the problem. A quick mental scan of every male she knew didn't turn up anyone who made her feel the way Sam did. She was so disconcerted by that thought, Jasmine's gasp took her completely by surprise.

Tabitha turned around. "What?"

"Your shirt."

"Huh?" But when she glanced down, she realized exactly what Jasmine meant. Not her shirt at all. Sam's shirt.

She hadn't taken it off last night, had slept in it, hugging her arms around her body, holding the shirt close to her skin. She didn't want to think about what that might signify.

"Look, I, um, well..."

"You had sex with Sam."

Tabitha winced at Jasmine's accusatory tone. She struggled for an answer, but in the end just shrugged.

"You're wearing his shirt. His lucky shirt."

"His lucky shirt?" She looked down dubiously at the worn blue cotton. He'd talked about his lucky shirt on the air before, but she'd always thought he was making it up. "This ratty old thing?"

Jasmine frowned, her eyes full of censure. "Tabitha, how could you?"

How could she what? Get pregnant? Sleep with Sam? Risk ruining the on-air dynamic of their show? Risk her career? Make an ass out of herself by bringing up marriage? Of course, she'd asked herself these same questions all night. She had no answers. Not for herself and certainly not for Jasmine.

She'd blown it big-time, and now all she could do was muddle through it the best she could.

"Look, I'm sorry," she offered automatically. Then she stopped herself. "Wait. Why am I apologizing to you? You're my friend—you're supposed to be supportive. Besides, ever since I broke up with Bob you've been telling me to cut loose a little. To find my blender."

"I meant that you should go dancing and maybe let a guy or two buy you a drink. I didn't mean you should have sex with Sam."

"Would you stop saying it that way? Jeez, it's not that big a deal. We just had sex. That's all. Let's not forget who's the veteran of office slap-and-tickle."

"That's different."

"How is it different? You and Roger from marketing used to sneak off during coffee breaks to have sex in the bathroom. At least I was at home where I wouldn't get caught. How could *this* possibly be worse?"

"It's worse because the show's success is based on the great chemistry—"

Oh, this was the last thing she needed to hear.

Tabitha threw up her hands. "Chemistry! Why is everyone suddenly talking about us having great chemistry? I don't even know what that means."

"Well, the listeners know. I guarantee it. You sizzle when you're on the air together."

"We don't sizzle. Fajitas sizzle."

Jasmine shook her head. "Don't be obtuse."

"I'm not being obtuse. I just don't believe there's some mysterious...whatever between Sam and I that makes the show great."

"Of course it's there. At least it was. Before you had sex. Who knows now."

"What's that supposed to mean?"

"Everybody knows chemistry disappears after a couple gets hooked up. Like Sam and Diane from 'Cheers.' Or Maddie and David on 'Moonlighting.' Or Lois and Clark."

"The explorers?"

"*Lois* and Clark, not *Lewis* and Clark. From the TV show."

"You're telling me I should base my life on a TV show?"

"Not just a TV show. It's a paradigm."

"A paradigm?" Tabitha asked doubtfully.

"Yes. A paradigm for how romances work. At least on TV shows. They start out with great chemistry between the two leads. They string the audience along, then when they finally give the audience what they want and the two leads get together, the audience loses interest and the show dies."

"And that's what you think is going to happen to our

show? You think that people are going to stop listening just because Sam and I had sex?"

"Well, yeah." Jasmine, the fatalist, nodded. "We're doomed."

"We are not doomed. Even if I believed in your ridiculous theory that the show's success is based on chemistry, which I don't, we would only be doomed if the listeners found out Sam and I had sex. They're not going to find out—therefore, we're not doomed."

"Oh, come on. You can't expect to hide your relationship forever."

"Relationship? We don't have a relationship. It was fling. A one-night stand."

Jasmine's eyebrows shot up. "A one-night stand?"

"Yes, a one-night stand. Why is that so hard to believe?"

Jasmine shrugged. "I just thought that with the kind of chemistry you two have, once wouldn't be enough."

"Would you please stop with the chemistry thing? There is no chemistry, no pizzazz, no sizzle. It was just sex. Plain, ordinary—" *earth-shattering* "—sex."

Jasmine's eyes widened in exaggerated doubt. "If you say so." Then she straightened as if suddenly remembering something important. "What are you going to do about your date?"

"What date?"

"Your date for the contest. And your blind date, for that matter. How are you going to get out of them?"

Tabitha considered for a minute, desperately trying to shove aside her careening emotions. "I'm not. I'll just go on both dates. It won't be that bad."

Jasmine grasped her hand. "Please tell me you're kidding."

Tabitha pulled her hand away. "I'm not kidding. I

have to do it. The blind date with Chandi's teacher is in just a few days. It's too late to cancel it. As for the date with—" she squeezed her eyes shut, searching her memory for the hapless listener's name "—with...Jim, well, it's the end of the contest. My final obligation."

"Jim? Who's Jim?"

She shot Jasmine a look of annoyance. "Jim is the listener I picked for the date."

"Not Newton Doyle?"

"No, not Newton Doyle." Newton Doyle was too tempting. Another complication in the already screwed-up mess she'd made of her life. "Jim, the actor."

"The guy who included his head shot with the love letter?"

"How did you know about that?"

"Sam passed it around the office. We all thought it was hysterical." She shook her head. "I can't believe you picked him. The listeners are going to be really pissed when they find out you dumped Sam to go out with a vain actor."

"You can stop worrying about what is or isn't going to upset the listeners, because the listeners will never know it happened. And you can forget it ever happened, because it will *not* happen again."

"What about Sam?"

"What about him?"

"What if he mentions it?"

"He won't."

"How can you be so sure?"

"Because if he does—" she slammed her mug on the counter "—I'll kill him."

11

SHE WAS IN TROUBLE. Serious trouble.

Her life was crumbling like a double-stuffed Oreo left too long in a glass of milk. Right now, she should be desperately fishing out the little bits of chocolate cookie and creamy center and trying to mash them back together.

What was she doing instead? She was sitting on her bed, fantasizing about having sex with Sam. Wild sex.

Sex with Sam was the last thing she should be fantasizing about. She should be fantasizing about having a painted nursery. Or preassembled baby furniture. Or a prearranged diaper service. Something—anything—productive.

Besides, Jasmine swore the chemistry would dissipate now that they'd had sex. But had it? No. Being around Sam still got her hot and bothered. Her fantasies were still hitting her in full force. She still had to fight the urge to back him against the studio wall and tear off his clothes.

And it certainly didn't help matters that her fantasies now weren't fueled solely by her imagination.

She'd spent the whole week feeling hyped up and tingly, unable to forget everything he'd said and done Friday night. Every time she'd looked at him, she'd remembered how he'd been: forceful, relentless, gentle.

It gave her goose bumps even now.

Yet, Sam had been oddly distant all week. He hadn't

said a single word about what had happened Friday night. Hadn't tried to touch or to kiss her. Or to back her up against the studio wall, pull her clothes off and—

Well, the less she dwelled on her own fantasies the better.

Tabitha sighed, scooted off the bed, then headed for her closet. In less than an hour she was supposed to meet Jonathon Romone for their date. Obsessing about Sam wasn't going to make this date any easier. But if she was going to obsess, she should at least dress while she was doing it.

She was reaching for her "indispensable" little black dress when she heard the doorbell ring.

Since she wasn't expecting anyone, she ignored it. It rang again. Then three more times in staccato bursts followed by one long blast before she made it to the door.

She flung it open without even bothering to look through the peephole. Only Sam could be this annoying.

"What?" she barked as soon as he stopped leaning on the doorbell.

He stood on her doorstep, wearing faded jeans and a T-shirt, this one green, holding a brown paper bag in one hand and a soda in the other. As he walked past her into the house, he pointed in her direction with the soda can. "Tell me you're not wearing that on your blind date."

"What?" Then she glanced down and realized she wore only her black silk slip. She slammed the door shut. "What are you doing here?"

He held up the bag. "I came to install window locks."

"What?" He shot her a look full of amused arrogance and she realized that she'd said what three times in row. Nothing like a radio professional with the vocabulary of a parrot. She took a deep breath that didn't expel any of

her nervousness. "Why are you here to install window
locks?"

"I got your window unlocked in less than thirty seconds. If I'd been a burglar or a rapist, you wouldn't have
even had the time to call the police."

"If you'd been a determined burglar or rapist, locks
wouldn't have kept you out, either."

"True." He crossed to her kitchen table, shoved aside
her flower vase, and then dumped the contents of the bag
onto the table. He spoke without looking at her, sorting
through the gadgets he'd brought. "This might buy you
some time." He looked up at her, his eyes darting first to
her face, then settling on her chest. "That *isn't* what
you're wearing, is it?"

"No, this is just my slip," she said before giving in to
the temptation to make sure nothing was showing that
shouldn't be. Her stance—hands propped on her hips—
stretched the silk of her slip tightly across her chest in a
way it never would have in her pre-baby days. She
dropped her arms, then crossed them before realizing
that posture accentuated them even more. Flustered and
defeated, she retreated to her bedroom. Sam followed.

He stood in the doorway, one arm propped against the
doorjamb, watching as she snagged her terry-cloth robe
and yanked it on.

Feeling only marginally better with a quarter inch of
fluffy cotton between her skin and Sam's gaze, she did
her best to face him without fidgeting.

After studying her for what felt like decades, he
stepped into the room and asked, "What *are* you wearing
tonight for you blind date?"

Instead of answering she pointed to the simple crepe
sheath. To her surprise, he crossed to where it hung on
the door and studied it before nodding. "Good. I

wouldn't have let you leave the house wearing what you had on."

The words were indisputably possessive. And the implication behind those words scared her. He cared what she wore. And he cared what other men saw her in.

And yet...when she opened her mouth, she found her defensiveness speaking for her. "You wouldn't have let me? What makes you think you have any say in what I wear?"

In two steps he'd crossed to stand in front of her. With an almost imperceptible touch, he ran his thumb along her cheek. "The same thing that makes me think that you'll spend all night remembering this."

He leaned down to kiss her.

If there had been even a second when she might have pulled away from him, it passed unnoticed. Any will to resist was overpowered by her need. Not just her need to taste him again, but her need to know.

Was the chemistry still there? Could Sam still make her ache with a single touch? If he did, how far would she let him go? How easy would it be to be that easy?

In the instant before his mouth touched hers, her lips curved in a smile, amused by her own pun. With her eyes closed, her lips tilted and her breath caught, she waited. For his lips. His touch. For insight and understanding.

For a kiss that never came.

Her eyes fluttered open. Confusion, annoyance and pure lust warred within her. He was close, so close. But he wasn't touching her. Wasn't kissing her. And, apparently, wasn't wanting her the way she wanted him.

"Humph," she muttered peevishly. "Well, you're going to have to do better than that."

He cocked an eyebrow, a smile teasing at his lips as he leaned infinitesimally closer. "Really?"

"What? You expect me to mope around all night remembering how you barged into my house, ordered me around, then just stood here, looming over me?"

His smile broadened to a full grin. "No." Unexpectedly she felt her robe being flicked open as his hand slipped inside to skim up her thigh, under her slip, over her panties, to rest high on her hip. "I expect you to mope around all night wondering what might have happened if you'd stayed here with me."

"WAIT!"

Sam smiled as he watched Tabitha in his rearview mirror. Her arms waving frantically, she stumbled after his car.

"Wait! Sam!"

He pressed his foot on the accelerator and drove past the next house before pretending just then to notice her chasing after him. He slammed on the brakes and screeched to a halt in front of her neighbor's house. He left his car running and jumped out.

"Tabitha? What's wrong?" he asked, oozing mock concern to hide his satisfaction. He'd timed this perfectly.

She stopped a few feet away, her breath coming in short little bursts, evidence of how much she'd exerted herself trying to catch him. Any annoyance he felt at the stress she'd subjected her body to was overpowered by his reaction at the sight of her.

God, she looked good. She wore the little black dress. Its full skirt ended just above her knees. It was loose enough that only the barest hint of the baby was noticeable. If he hadn't known better, he just would have thought she'd been hitting the junk food too hard.

But he did know better. He knew how soft the skin of her belly felt under his fingertips. He knew how tender her breasts were. And he knew how frightened she was of going through this alone.

That last thought was *almost* enough to make him feel guilty about tampering with her car.

"What's wrong?" he asked again.

She gestured vaguely in the direction of her driveway without taking her eyes off him. "My car won't start."

Relieved that she didn't appear suspicious, he frowned. "You want me to take a look at it?"

She glanced at her watch. "No. I'm running late already. Can you just drop me off at the radio station?"

"You're meeting your date at the station?"

"It seemed neutral. If it's a disaster, I don't want him knowing where I live. So can you drop me off on your way home?"

Damn! He should have predicted she'd want a ride instead of help fixing her car. This was Tabitha, after all. When was the last time she'd been late for anything?

"You sure you don't want me to take a look at it?"

She nodded, glancing nervously at her watch.

He thought he'd timed this whole thing to maximize the delay, giving him time to tinker with her car, maybe put the distributor cap back on—after all, he didn't want her mechanic pointing out that distributor caps don't just pop off. She'd still be late enough that the history professor would give up and go back to his pathetic little university life.

Now Tabitha's compulsive promptness had screwed up everything. He growled his frustration. "We wouldn't want the professor to think you'd stood him up, now would we?"

"Can you take me or not?"

He exhaled slowly, trying to rid himself of his jealousy. "Get in."

She frowned, gave him a look that bordered on suspicion, then crossed behind his car to the passenger door. As she slid in beside him, she glanced at him and asked, "What's your problem?"

"I don't have a problem." He bit out the words, but didn't look at her, didn't want her to see the furious pace of his thoughts as he scrambled for a new delay.

"Fine." She stiffened, then shifted to stare out the window. "Just get me there, okay?"

He stomped on the clutch, slammed into first gear, and peeled away, taking more than a little satisfaction in her surprised little shriek.

"In one piece!"

He glanced over to see her frantically clutching at the door with one hand and fumbling for her seat belt with the other. "Hmm?"

"In one piece. Please get me there in one piece."

He barely slowed down as he turned off her road onto the development's major thoroughfare.

"Jeez, slow down!"

He immediately pressed the clutch, letting his car coast. "I thought you didn't want to be late."

"I don't want to be dead, either."

"Lighten up."

"Look, I know you like to be Mr. Cavalier, but I don't want this piece of junk falling apart around us."

He ignored the slight against his car. He knew she looked like a clunker, but beneath her dozens of dents and scratches beat the heart of a high-performance stock car. She handled like a dream. And he knew how to handle her. At least he knew how to handle one of the females in his life.

"Don't worry. I know the limits of this car." He

glanced at Tabitha in time to see her roll her eyes. "Besides, I would never put you in danger."

I would never put you in danger? Where the hell had *that* come from? And did it sound as dumb as he thought? He'd never said anything that sappy before. For that matter, he doubted if any real man had.

He almost didn't hear Tabitha when she said, "I know."

He looked over at her again as he turned his car onto the Capital of Texas Highway. "Huh?"

"I know you wouldn't put me in danger." She paused, then went on in a rush. "I've just been really high strung lately. I don't know what's wrong with me."

He cocked an eyebrow. "Really? Maybe I can take a guess."

She blushed. "I mean, besides the obvious. This isn't like me. You know that. And I shouldn't have complained about your car. Especially since I wouldn't have made it in time without a ride."

Boy, did she know how to lay on the guilt. Of course, she didn't *know* she was laying on the guilt, because she didn't know that she wouldn't have needed a ride if he hadn't tampered with her car.

He battled with his guilt up to the moment he turned into the station parking lot. The lot was practically empty. After all, the employees of the other businesses sharing the building worked mostly Monday through Friday. He recognized the few cars that belonged to the station's weekend staff. But, parked at the far end of the lot, angled across three spaces to prevent other cars from parking near it, was a car he'd never seen before. A car that had to belong to the history professor. A coal-black, 1992 Aston Martin. Just like James Bond used to drive.

"Looks like your date's over there." He had to force a

light tone in the words. He didn't want to pretend that he didn't care she was going out on this date. But he didn't know what else to do. She'd turned him down flat, his plan to sabotage her car had backfired, and now he was supposed to just hand her over to this guy?

Short of kidnapping, he didn't see that he had much choice.

Just then, Tabitha groaned. Not a groan of pain, which would have scared him to death, but her little annoyed groan. "Ick. A little sports car. I should have known." For reasons he couldn't even begin to understand, she turned and glared at him, as if this was somehow his fault.

"You don't like sports cars?" he asked hopefully.

She rolled her eyes. "Too much testosterone. He probably also wears three-hundred-dollar sunglasses and drives like a sixteen-year-old boy." Then she reached for the door handle.

Unfortunately, Mr. Aston Martin got there before she did. The guy opened the door and extended his hand.

"You must be Tabitha," he said in a clipped English accent.

She shot Sam one last look, eyebrow arched sarcastically, before placing her hand in the stranger's and allowing herself to be eased from the car.

The passenger door swung closed, cutting off any chance Sam had of hearing her response. He fumed in silence for a second, contemplating his choices, then got out of the car and rounded the back in time to catch the tail end of the introduction.

Tabitha looked at him, clearly surprised he hadn't just driven off, then shrugged and gestured in his direction. "Well, Sam was nice enough to offer to drive me here."

Mr. Aston Martin smiled thankfully and nodded. "Well there, chap, that was certainly sporting of you."

Chap? Sporting? Did the English really talk like this? "Just helping out a friend."

His irritation must have come out in his voice because Tabitha frowned at him before bestowing on Jonathon an overly warm smile. "I'm going to run upstairs for a minute. I'll be right back."

Jonathon assured her he didn't mind, smiling amiably until Tabitha was out of sight. As soon as she disappeared into the building, however, the charming facade began to crumble.

He turned to Sam. "So man, tell me about Tabitha."

The thick English accent had faded a bit, giving Sam the impression that, although it might be genuine, the guy had definitely beefed it up for Tabitha because he knew women liked it.

The lecherous smile, the disappearing accent, and the flashy sports car said it all. The guy was an asshole. A predatory one at that.

Her date could have been a wheelchair-bound, ninety-seven-year-old, Nobel Peace prize recipient and Sam wouldn't have wanted her to go. But this guy? This cocky, English asshole? There was no way Sam was going to stand by and let this guy get his hands on Tabitha.

He was going to have to come up with something. Buying himself some time, he asked, "What do you want to know?"

"Anything that'll be helpful."

"Helpful how?" Sam snarled the words even though he knew exactly what the guy meant. He just wanted to hear it out loud before he beat the crap out of him.

Jonathon's smile slipped, as if he heard the barely restrained anger in Sam's voice. "Helpful...getting to know her. You know, what she likes and doesn't.... That kind of thing."

Okay, so he wasn't as dumb as he looked. But Sam wasn't, either. If he decked the guy now, Sam would end up looking like the bad guy and Jonathon would get all the sympathy.

Sam stared at the guy for a second, contemplating his options. Finally he said, "You want to know what she likes? What will really impress her?" Jonathon nodded. "You ever read *Wuthering Heights*?"

12

"DON'T ASK." Tabitha waved aside her friend's questions and slumped into her chair.

Jasmine, hovering beside Tabitha's desk, ignored the order. "What do you mean, don't ask? Of course I'm going to ask. What happened? How did it go? Why don't you want me to ask? What—"

"Stop, stop! Have a little mercy." Sitting up, she brushed the hair off her forehead with the back of her hand and glanced surreptitiously around the room. Luckily none of the other deejays were around. Sam sat at his desk a few feet away, but he barely glanced up. At least, only Sam and Jasmine would hear the tale of her humiliation.

Jasmine frowned. "Give me the dirt."

"There's no dirt. The date went...fine." She must have hesitated too long because Jasmine's eyes lit up and Sam nudged his chair away from his desk, leaned back, and crossed his arms over his stomach.

"Only fine?" he asked.

"Come on," Jasmine prodded. "I want details."

"There are no details." She shrugged. "Just normal first-date stuff."

"I'm waiting." Jasmine tapped the toe of her platform shoe, making little click-click noises on the linoleum.

Tabitha tried to force her lips into a smile, but stopped when Jasmine frowned suspiciously. Giving up, she propped her elbows on her desk and let her chin drop into her waiting hands. "Oh, God, it was horrible."

Jasmine's frown faded into sympathetic concern. "What went wrong?"

"False advertising. That's what went wrong. Jonathon said we were going to some boring film festival. Then after dinner—during which he nearly bored me to death talking about his troubled childhood—he changed his mind about the movies."

"So?" Sam asked, his lips twitching with what might have been a smile.

"He took me to a karaoke bar. Austin is the live music capital of the world. But did he take me to Antone's? No. Lazona Rosa? No. Any one of the hundred-and-fifty places you can hear live music on any given night? No, he took me to a karaoke bar."

"Oh." Jasmine's concern now held a note of distaste. "Well, that doesn't sound so bad."

"He took the mike not long after we got there and started singing me old Jimmy Buffett songs."

"Well, you're his date."

"At one point he dropped to his knees in front of me singing 'Margaritaville.' He refused to give up the mike. The management kicked us out." She rubbed her hands over her eyes, trying to block out her memories. "I've never been kicked out of any place in my life. I was so humiliated."

Jasmine winced. "That *does* sound bad."

"I don't know what went wrong. Chandi likes him. He sounded perfectly normal on the phone. I never had any hint that behind his polite veneer hid a neurotic Jimmy Buffett fan."

Jasmine clucked sympathetically. "Yeah, sometimes you just can't see it coming."

"Is this normal in the dating world?" she asked no one in particular.

The expression on Sam's face surprised her. The twitching lips had expanded into a definite grin and the gleam in his eyes was almost...well, almost self-satisfied.

"It's a statistical fact," Jasmine said. "According to a recent survey in *Cosmo*, over thirty percent of the single male population is undatable. So, yeah, every once in a while you'll get someone a little weird."

"A little? The date was so bad, it couldn't have gone worse if I'd planned it."

As soon as the words were out of her mouth, the pieces started falling into place. When she'd run upstairs to the rest room, she'd left Sam alone with Jonathon.

Her eyes found his and she stared at him for a long, silent moment as she thought it through, bit by bit. She wouldn't have been sure of it if Sam hadn't gotten nervous and looked away.

"You...you slimy little..."

"Huh?" Jasmine looked from one to the other in utter confusion.

Sam didn't even bother to look confused. He held up his hands in mock surrender and said, "Now, come on. It's not what you think."

"Oh? So you didn't deliberately sabotage my date?"

He shrugged. "I, um..."

She had to get out of here. Now.

In a flash, she'd gone from angry enough to knock Sam over the head with a two-by-four to ready to sink to the floor in tears. Well, she wouldn't give him the satisfaction of seeing her cry. He'd abused that privilege once already. Without looking at Sam or Jasmine, she grabbed her purse from the bottom drawer of her desk and headed for the door.

Sam watched Tabitha storm out without a word. Too late, he realized he should have stopped her. "Tabitha, wait!"

He hesitated, then glanced at Jasmine. She gave him one of her "men are dumb" looks and waved him in Tabitha's direction. "Go after her."

He caught her as she was stepping into the elevator. Ignoring the two businessmen in the back of the car, he braced a hand on the closing door, forcing it to open.

"Don't go like this. Give me a chance to explain."

With her arms crossed over her chest and her expression tired, she shrugged. "Okay, explain."

"Will you get off the elevator?"

"No."

The two suits shot confused glances at each other then at him. "Get off so we can talk about this. You're holding up the elevator."

"How considerate of you to worry about their schedule. By all means, let's get this over quickly. I only need to know one thing. Why did you do it?"

The men looked from Tabitha to him, awaiting his answer. The elevator began to beep at him, as if annoyed at being held up too long. And Tabitha watched him with a steady expectant gaze.

Finally he said the only thing he could think of. "I don't know."

"Perfect. Then why are you here? Why did you even stop me? You don't want me, but you don't want anyone else to have me, either. Well, you can't have it both ways."

The elevator dinged at him like the buzzer ticking off the time at a game show. Unable to think of anything to defend himself, he turned the tables on her. "What about you, Tabitha? If I can't have it both ways, then neither can you. What is it *you* want? You keep pressing me for a commitment, but we both know that if Bob showed up right now, you'd take him back before the door even shut behind him."

"I'm pressing you for a commitment? Hardly!"

"Last week in your bedroom, you were practically begging for a wedding ring."

"I didn't want a wedding ring. I wanted you gone."

"That sure wasn't what it sounded like at the time."

"Trust me, Sam. The only thing I want from you right now is your absence."

"Fine." He pulled his foot away from the door to let it close, but before it could, Tabitha stuck her hand out and held it open.

"Oh, and one other thing. Butt out of my life. What happens or doesn't happen next weekend during the blind date is none of your business. I swear, if you do anything to mess it up, the whole town will hear about it on the air the next morning."

His gray eyes flashed with anger. "I wouldn't dream of interfering after this. If you want to be left at the mercy of assholes, that's fine by me."

She nodded, her expression blank. "Fine."

Almost as if to punctuate her agreement, the elevator stopped beeping and let out one long wailing note. A final warning, he supposed. Game over.

She stepped back and let the doors slide shut. He stood staring at his own smudged reflection in the brushed stainless-steel doors. Why did he feel as out of focus as his reflection looked?

Slowly he turned and made his way back to his desk. Jasmine looked up in surprise. "You didn't catch her?"

He ignored the question, focusing instead on grabbing

his stuff, hoping to make a quick exit. He wasn't up to one of Jasmine's legendary interrogations.

"Sam?"

"Huh?"

Her eyes narrowed. "Did you catch her?"

He gave up and sank into his chair. "I caught her. I just didn't know what to do with her."

She rolled her chair a little closer to his and gave an exasperated sigh. "The man spends his radio life making love to his audience but doesn't know what to say to the woman he loves."

His head jerked up. "I don't love Tabitha."

"Of course, you do."

"No. I don't."

Jasmine gave him a long speculative look, then shrugged. "Okay. So you don't love Tabitha. But—"

Annoyed at being placated, he cut her off. "I really don't." Did he? Was that what this was all about?

"Fine." She brushed aside his insistence with a wave of sparkling fingertips. "You don't love her, but you do care about her, at least enough to not want her to see other men."

"You didn't meet this guy. He was a real ass."

Jasmine nodded. "Because you're jealous."

"No," he answered automatically, even though he was beginning to doubt himself.

Her smile broadened. "My point is, if you don't want to lose her, you need to act fast. She's very vulnerable right now. You don't want some guy with a nice turn of phrase coming in off the street and stealing her out from under you."

"Nobody's going to steal her out from under me because she's not under me at all." Figuratively speaking, of course.

"Well—" Jasmine gave a coy little wink "—maybe she should be."

"HEY, SAM, wake up."

Sam swatted at the hand shaking him awake, but the annoying hand just moved to another spot.

"Wake up."

Again, Sam tried to shake it off. Then he woke enough to realize he shouldn't have to swat anyone away in the middle of the night. He jerked upright in his bed, and his eyes flew open as he fumbled for the bedside lamp.

Finally his blurred gaze fell on Newt, who stood beside his bed, laptop in hand.

"What the hell are you doing in my room in the middle of night?"

"It's only ten-thirty."

Sam glanced sideways at the clock. Newt was right. Ten-thirty. Damn, it felt later than that.

Rubbing the grit from his eyes, he asked, "What are you doing here?"

Newt held up the laptop. "Tabitha's online. She's been IM-ing me. She wants to talk to you."

"What's she doing?"

"IM-ing me—Instant Messaging me."

Jealousy settled into Sam's gut like a bad pizza eaten too late at night. He flopped back onto the bed. "So answer her."

"She doesn't want to talk to me. I'm just a name to her."

Sam propped himself up on his elbows to study his friend. "Don't you want to talk to her?"

Newt shrugged. "Nah. Sure, she's hot, but I don't even know what to say to her. Besides, I've been chatting online with Jasmine. She's pretty cool."

As Sam watched, a blush crept through Newt's pale skin. "And Tabitha wants the guy who wrote her that letter. The guy she spent an hour online with last week. She wants you."

"Trust me, I am the last thing Tabitha wants right now."

"Whatever. You know her better than I do." Newton started to leave, then said, "I was wondering about something, though."

"What?"

"If you're so in love with Tabitha, why did you try to help me get a date with her?"

"I'm not in love with Tabitha."

Newt ignored his protest. "I mean, it's pretty obvious that she and I wouldn't work out. Sure, she's hot, but she's not really my type."

Sam blinked, trying to clear his mind to process at least a single thought. "You have a type?"

"Then it hit me. You didn't want it to work out. She had to go out with someone, so you picked me 'cause you knew it wouldn't work."

He protested automatically, "That's not—"

"No, man, it's cool. It all worked out. I met Jasmine, right? But, dude, you need to come clean. You need to tell her you love her."

"I'm not in love with Tabitha." Why was everyone so sure he loved Tabitha?

"Oh. Then why was it so important to you that she like the letters?"

"I just… It was…" He punched at his pillow. "Damn it, I'm not in love with her."

"Okay. Whatever, man." Newton set the laptop down on Sam's nightstand. "Use it if you want. The program is up and running. All you need to do is answer her."

Newton turned to leave, but Sam sat up and called, "Hey, how'd you get in?"

"I still had your house key from when you went out of town last summer."

"I didn't give it to you so you could break into my house in the middle of the night."

Newt shrugged. "I know, but it was an emergency." His lips curved into a smile. "When it's important, you use whatever you've got."

Sam flopped back onto the bed and stared at his ceiling. Newt's words rang in his head. *When it's important, you use whatever you've got....*

Was Newt right? Had he offered to help him knowing Tabitha would never fall for the guy?

He pressed the heels of his hands against his eyes. What the hell had he been thinking?

Of course Tabitha wasn't going to fall in love with Newt. They had nothing in common. Tabitha was quick-witted and articulate. Newt could barely string together a couple of lucid sentences. Newt programmed computers for a living, Tabitha couldn't program her VCR. Newt was a great guy, but Sam couldn't imagine Tabitha falling for him. Not in a million years.

Sam had other friends. Handsome, successful buddies. Guys he could imagine Tabitha falling for. A couple of them, he knew, had even entered letters in the contest. But he hadn't helped any of them write her letters. No, he'd tried to hook her up with the geeky computer programmer. It didn't take a genius to figure out why.

He was in love in Tabitha. And, frankly, it had knocked him on his ass and turned him into a complete idiot.

He could only hope that in trying to make sure she didn't fall in love with anyone else, he hadn't ruined any chance of her falling in love with him. In the past couple of weeks he'd bullied her, lied to her and misled her. Once he came clean about Newton Doyle, he'd be lucky if she ever wanted to see him again.

Unless...

Unless she never found out he was Newton.

Maybe Newton could just disappear.

But what if she kept e-mailing him? What if she wouldn't let him bow out?

Irrational jealousy surged through him. What the hell was she doing e-mailing Newton in the middle of the night anyway? What was up with that?

Served him right. He wanted to write a letter she wouldn't be able to forget. Well, he had. Now he had to deal with it.

Okay, since he had to deal with the possibility that she wouldn't let Newton fade away, could he use Newton to his advantage?

Could he be any less ethical?

He stared at the laptop, then rolled over, pretended for about five seconds that he was trying to go back to sleep. But Newton's words kept echoing in his mind. *When it's important, you use whatever you've got.* He sat up. Pulling the computer onto his lap, he released the catch and raised the lid. A few seconds later he was staring at her message to Newt.

"Hey, Two-Stepping Guy, do you want to talk?"

"Sure."

There was a long pause and he wondered if she'd already gone offline.

Then she wrote, "I thought you were ignoring me."

He'd tried. Damn it, he'd been trying for years. Shaking his head at his own blasted stupidity, he typed, "I could never ignore you."

"I'm glad."

Her words rankled. Apparently she had no problem ignoring him. She'd ignored him at work every day for what felt like weeks. Years. On the air, everything was just as it had always been. But the minute they walked out the studio door, it was as though he didn't even exist.

He couldn't say any of that without giving himself away. So he wrote, "You're up late."

"You know what time I go to bed?"

Nine o'clock. Ten-thirty on weekends. "I just assumed radio personalities all went to bed early."

"Normally, I do. I couldn't sleep tonight."

Her words brought forth the image of her in bed, tangled in the pristine white sheets, restlessly chasing sleep. He squeezed his eyes shut against the image, but he couldn't banish it.

"Aren't you going to ask why I couldn't sleep?"

"Okay. Why couldn't you sleep?"

"I keep thinking about what you said the last time we talked online. That a girl can be *too* careful. Were you talking in general or about me specifically?"

He tapped his fingers lightly against the keys while thinking about how to respond. Ultimately he admitted, "You specifically."

"You don't even know me."

Her defensiveness didn't surprise him. "I know you better than you think."

"Listening to the show every morning doesn't make you an expert."

No, but being with her every day gave him some insight. "Just trust me on this."

"Newton isn't your real name, is it?"

The moment of truth. If he lied, he'd essentially be giving her back to Newt. Even if he told her the truth, he couldn't tell her the whole truth. She was pissed off at him as it was. But he wasn't giving her up. "No, it's not."

"What is your real name?"

"Does it really matter?"

"Yes."

"I'm not some deranged sicko, if that's what you're worried about."

"Would you tell me if you were a deranged sicko?"

"I'll tell you anything you want to know about me, except my real name."

"But that's what I want to know."

"Or I can tell you about yourself."

"Since you're such an expert?"

"Exactly." He didn't wait for her reply. "You're stronger than you think, Tabitha. You don't have to be so afraid of being weak, of needing people. You can cut loose every once in while. You don't always have to be the responsible adult."

"If I don't, then who will be?"

"You have friends, people who care about you, who will step up and take care of you if you'll let them."

"People like you, Newton?"

"No." He suppressed a twinge of bitterness and a twisted form of jealousy toward "Newton." He, Sam, wanted to take care of her but she'd already made it clear she didn't think he was capable. "People in your real life. Whatever it is that's keeping you up at night, you can handle it. But you don't have to handle it on your own. You can ask for help."

That's when it hit him. He'd been forcing her to accept his help for too long. From here on out, she'd have to ask.

Only he'd spent so much effort to get her back to the Tough-as-Nails Tabitha, and now that she was, she would never ask for help.

13

THIS REALLY SUCKED.

It was Saturday night, date night all over the United States, and he was stuck at home. His lounger, no matter how comfortable, couldn't make up for the fact that Tabitha—his Tabitha—was out on a date with another man while he watched *Lethal Weapon* on cable for the thirteenth time.

He didn't care that this date with Jim was just part of her job. He didn't even care that she'd obviously been reluctant even to go.

What he did care about was that she'd picked Jim instead of Newton.

Irrational? Yep.

Jealous? Yep.

Happy about it? Nope.

He frowned at the television, then fumbled for a second for the remote control, clicking just as Gibson opened fire.

"The lioness, pride of the African veldt..." The camera focused in on a lion while the voice-over droned on.

And why was he stuck at home? He clicked again.

"You could be driving—" Click.

He didn't know. He could have at least called up a couple of buddies and gone to that billiards place down the block. Anything would have been better than this.

"In department stores, you'd pay—" Click.

But he was sitting at home, torturing himself with visions of Tabitha…on a moonlit dinner cruise down Town Lake…with Jim.

"If Rogers doesn't make this shot—" Click.

Jim. The handsome, buff type.

"Guaranteed to—" Click, click.

Jim, who'd gone to Julliard, for Pete's sake.

"Then brutally murdered his girlfriend—" Click, click, click.

Jim, who'd just been on TV.

Sam jerked forward, sending the footrest of his lounger snapping back into place. He smashed his thumb down on the channel button with such force the remote spun from his hand, tumbling onto the chair arm and then to the floor. He leaped from the chair, grabbed the remote and pounded the buttons until the TV responded. He clicked furiously until he found the station then sank, dumbfounded, into the chair behind him as he watched.

"The killing spree ended two days later when police arrested both men in this L.A. apartment."

A grainy, news stock clip showed two men being led, handcuffed, toward a row of squad cars angled around a dingey apartment building. The camera focused on the face of the first man, then panned to the second. Jim.

Sam watched the screen intently, hoping—no, praying—he'd been wrong, but the man on screen ducked his head, then turned to stare directly into the camera through dead, heartless eyes.

That man on screen was Jim… Jim… Jim… Damn it, what was his last name?

The clip ended and the show switched to a shot of the host in "America's Most Dangerous Criminals" headquarters. "When we come back, you'll hear how these two brutal murderers escaped from custody. But if you already know where Michael Stalfast or Chris Benson are hiding—" mug shots of the two men appeared on screen "—call the number at the bottom of the screen. Our telephone operators are waiting for your call."

Sam grabbed his phone and dialed the last digit just as the number faded away. The phone rang. Once... twice...then picked up before the third ring.

"Thank God, I've got—"

"Your information is important to us. If you're calling about a criminal on tonight's show, please press or say one now—"

He hung up and hurled the phone onto the sofa. Damn it!

He paced, furious and terrified, wondering what he should do. If he called the police, would they believe him?

Probably not.

He glanced at his watch. Twelve after eight. The moonlit cruise was to leave at eight-thirty. That gave him eighteen minutes to get down to the lake.

Saving Tabitha was up to him.

TABITHA TRIED TO SMILE through her white-knuckled fear.

Jim smiled, oblivious of the way she clenched the dashboard. "Don't worry about this traffic. I'll get us there in time. It's a good thing the limo's tire went out so close to the station and I was able to walk back and get my car. If we'd had to wait for the replacement, we never would have made it to the dock on time," he said as the car shot across two lanes of traffic. He didn't seem to hear the five successive horn blasts criticizing his maneuvering.

She, on the other hand, held her breath, waiting for the sound of crunching metal.

"This is nothing compared to the traffic in L.A. Besides—" he flashed her a big smile "—I played a race-car driver in my last movie."

Through gritted teeth she asked, "Did you drive the race cars in the movie?"

"No. All the driving was done by stunt drivers, but I had a great death scene."

She stopped listening. She didn't feel guilty. As long as she kept smiling and nodding, Jim probably wouldn't even notice. Who was she kidding? She could probably throw open the car door and leap into oncoming traffic and Jim probably wouldn't notice.

When she'd first read the description of this date, it had sounded great—like the kind of date Newton would come up with. The moonlit cruise on Town Lake...a benefit for a local charity, catered by a restaurant she'd always wanted to try, but never had because it was too expensive...live music by one of her favorite bands. It had sounded wonderful. Romantic. Perfect.

Oh, how wrong she'd been.

And this guy was ruining their date all on his own. He hadn't had the "benefit" of any coaching from Sam. She'd made sure they'd never even met. Though Sam had been in the office the day Jim came up to introduce himself and to finalize the plans, she'd made sure to steer him clear of Sam. No, this guy was doing all the damage himself.

She was still mentally listing all the things she'd rather be doing—had made it all the way down to volunteering for medical research—when Jim pulled the car to a stop in front of the restaurant from which the boat was leaving. The valet rushed to her door, eager to help her from the car.

She and Jim were at the restaurant door when she heard squealing tires and turned in time to see a car peel into the parking lot. The car jumped the curb, flattened a bush and screeched to a halt behind Jim's car.

Her heart skipped a beat when she recognized the car—and the driver.

She spun on her heel and stormed into the restaurant, dragging Jim along behind her.

"Tabitha—"

She heard Sam call out just as the door closed behind them. She didn't stop. In fact, she sped up, weaving her way through the bar, past the hostess's table, and straight through the dining room toward the back deck.

She wasn't about to let Sam ruin this for her. Not that there was much he could do to top Jim's efforts.

"Tabitha, wait!" Sam called from somewhere behind her.

Throughout the restaurant, heads turned to look at Sam, who was fast approaching...running actually.

Jim tugged on her arm. "I think someone's calling you."

Oh, you think? By now they were out the back door and headed across the restaurant deck toward the dock. Suddenly she just didn't want Sam to win this round.

"Ignore him," she ordered.

"But he's calling you."

Jim pulled on her arm, stopping her effectively, because, even if she made a dash for the boat, she couldn't get on without the tickets he held. A quick glance over her shoulder showed her Sam had been stopped by one of the waiters.

She turned to Jim. "Look, can we just get on the boat? I really don't want to talk to that man."

"But don't you know him? I thought he was your cohost."

"He's not."

"Then why is his picture next to yours on billboards all over town?"

Damn! "Well..." *Think, Tabitha, think!* "They just hired that guy to pose with me for the billboards because...the real Sam was horribly disfigured...when his cell phone exploded."

Ugh! Where had that come from? Cell phones didn't explode. No one, not even Jim, would believe they did. She glanced at Jim, waiting for the inevitable doubt to cloud his perfect features.

Instead he went pale. His gaze darted suspiciously to the cell phone he wore clipped to his belt. "My God, it ruined his face? That's horrible!"

"Yes! It was. The real Sam doesn't even go out in public anymore."

"But why is this guy following you around? And why don't you want to see him?"

"I don't know." She tried to pull him further across the deck, but Jim wouldn't budge. Finally she blurted, "Maybe he's stalking me."

"Stalking you?"

"Yeah, he's been following me around for months now. I can't get him to leave me alone."

Jim's forehead furrowed in an artful display of concern. "Have you contacted the police?"

Seconds passed while she tried to think of an answer. Of course, if someone was stalking her, she would have contacted the police. "No," she answered a little sheepishly. "I will, though. But for tonight let's just ignore him. Let's make it to the boat and forget we ever saw him."

She grabbed hold of Jim's hand and pulled him toward the boat and the small group of people waiting to board. Maybe she could blend.

Just as she reached the dock, Jim stopped her again.

"It's not a good idea to ignore him. He could be dangerous. This isn't something to take lightly. I know. I played a stalker once in the TV movie *Love's Dangerous Obsession*."

Of course! Of course, he'd played a stalker. Why hadn't she seen that one coming? "Believe me. I take this as seriously as it deserves."

Jim puffed out his chest and went on in a voice reminiscent of the read-more-about-it announcements that usually followed TV movies. "You should contact the police to file a report. And you should tell this man unequivocally you don't want to see or talk to him."

"I'll do that," she agreed eagerly, hoping he'd drop it. She turned to go. Again he stopped her.

"Maybe I should talk to him. After all, I once played a—"

"A what? A psychologist? A cop? A hostage negotiator?"

Jim pulled back, either confused or hurt. "A bodyguard."

Before she could apologize, or even decide if she should give him that much encouragement, Sam reached them.

He skidded to a stop several feet away. "I need to talk to you, Tabitha." He held out his hand to her, entreating her with his eyes.

Jim stepped in front of her, blocking Sam's way. "Tabitha, get on the boat. I'll handle this."

She didn't go to the boat. She didn't need Jim handling anything for her. She was long past regretting every lie she'd told him. He seemed to be taking her stalker pretty seriously, which was the last thing she wanted.

"Wait," Sam called. "Don't go with him, Tabby. He's not who he says he is."

"She doesn't want to see you and she'll call the police if you follow her again."

"What?" Sam asked, clearly surprised and confused. And why wouldn't he be? She'd made a horrible mess of this whole thing.

A glance over her shoulder in the direction of the boat told her they were attracting an audience. A glance up toward the restaurant confirmed it. She had to put an end to this before someone really did call the police and they were all arrested.

She placed a hand on Jim's arm to nudge him out of the way. "Neither of you—"

Jim's arm shot out, holding her back. Before she could shrug off his protection, Sam rushed forward.

"Let her go, you bastard!"

She stepped out of Jim's grasp just before Sam tackled him. The force of the impact propelled both men down to the dock. Tabitha barely jumped aside as they landed with a loud thump at her feet. For a second time stopped and they all three froze as if the impact had knocked the life from them.

Then the spell broke.

Sam jerked his head up and yelled, "Run, Tabitha! Run to safety."

Jim bucked beneath Sam, gaining enough leverage to punch him. Sam's head snapped back. She yelped involuntarily and leaped aside.

Whatever advantage surprise had given Sam, he soon lost. As big as Sam was, Jim was bigger. Add to that the martial arts training he'd bragged about earlier and he had a clear advantage. All this flashed through her mind as she watched Sam and Jim struggle for dominance. Jim rolled them both over, whacking Sam's head against the wood with a resounding crack.

She winced, but managed to contain a squeal. She

didn't know anything about fighting, but surely Sam couldn't take much of this. And she certainly wasn't going to stand by like some bimbo in a horror flick—the kind that watched people getting slashed but did nothing useful
to help.

She looked behind, appealing to the crowd for help. None of the shocked customers managed to tear their eyes from the action. She turned to the maître d' and ordered, "Do something!"

"I've already called the police. They're on their way."

Oh, great. The police. Just what she needed. What had Sam gotten them into this time?

Well, that was it. Saving Sam was up to her.

If only so she could kill him when this was all over with. She stepped closer. "Sam, watch out!"

"Tabby, stay back! For God's sake, he could be carrying a gun!" Sam shouted.

"A gun?" Jim arched back in surprise, giving Sam enough room to land a punch. Jim cried out in pain. "My face! Don't—"

A second punch cut him off. Apparently, Jim was much more interested in defending his precious face than he had been in defending her, because he attacked Sam with renewed vigor.

They rolled once, then again, stopping precariously close to the edge and the open water that lay beyond. Together, locked in violent parody of an embrace, they rocked side to side. Terrified they may fall in the water and hoping to end this stupid, senseless explosion of testosterone, Tabitha reached out, grabbing for their arms.

Simultaneously both men shook her off. Unbalanced, she fell on her behind with a painful thud.

Sam's head jerked up and stared at her through eyes

filled with concern. "Tabby." He choked out her name. "Oh, God. I'm sorry."

Anger spiraled through her. *Now* he was sorry? *Now?* After everything he'd done to her?

Oh, he was sorry all right. He was the sorriest excuse of a human she'd ever seen. And Jim ran a close second.

Suddenly too fed up even to watch them fight, she aimed one foot at Sam's shoulder and the other at Jim's. Then she pushed, rolling them both over the edge and into the water.

"AN ACTOR?" Sam asked, incredulous, as he climbed out of the police car.

"Yep." The officer unlocked the handcuffs with a flick of a key.

"In the dramatization?"

"Yep."

"An actor?" he repeated, still trying to absorb the enormity of his mistake.

"Well, buddy, you're not the first guy to turn in someone he knew." The cop shrugged. "Most interesting citizen's arrest I've seen, though."

Sam rolled his shoulders, stretching out the kinks that had formed while he'd sat, hands cuffed behind his back, crammed into the back of a cop car for the longest forty-five minutes of his life while the police checked Jim's story. His wet shirt clung to his back and his jeans were already starting to stiffen with lake scum.

"What would you have done if you'd thought your—" Sam broke off, looked over to where Tabitha stood talking to one of the cops "—your girlfriend was out with one of 'America's Most Dangerous Criminals'?"

"I wouldn't have let her go out with some other guy in the first place."

Easier said than done. As if he had any control over Tabitha.

As he watched, Tabitha headed toward the maître d', who hovered near the restaurant's front door, no doubt to make sure none of them sneaked back in.

Sam turned toward the cop. "Am I done here?"

"Yeah. Just don't watch so much TV."

When he caught up with Tabitha, she gave him an exasperated glare, then turned to the maître d'. "Can you call me a cab?"

"Jim's not taking you home?" Sam asked.

"Jim is on his way to the hospital so he can have a plastic surgeon stitch up his lip. Jim doesn't want to have anything to do with us 'crazy people'—at least, I think those were the words he screamed at me as he drove away. And if we're lucky, Jim won't sue the station for reckless endangerment or emotional trauma or whatever. So, no, Jim's not driving me home." She turned back to the maître d'. "Can you call me a cab? Yes or no?"

"Of course, ma'am."

"Let me take you home," Sam offered.

Tabitha shot him a look that said she'd rather walk over a bed of hot coals. To the maître d', she said, "Thanks. I'll wait out here. And again, I'm sorry."

Without so much as another glance in his direction, she walked to one of the benches.

"Hold off a minute on calling that cab, okay?" Sam said to the maître d' before following her.

She didn't look up when he settled down beside her, but instead just sat there, shoulders stiff, legs primly crossed, eyes staring blankly at the parking lot. Something about her posture spoke of exhaustion. And vulnerability. He fought the urge to pull her onto his lap and simply hold her in his arms.

Of course, that was probably the last thing she wanted.

Baby, Be Mine

He couldn't blame her. Ever since finding out Jim was an actor, not a serial killer, he'd felt like the biggest jerk alive. Yet how could he regret what he'd done? Truth was, he would run to her defense a hundred times and make a fool of himself every one of them if it meant keeping her safe.

The problem was, right now, he was the last person she wanted rushing to her defense. In fact he was fairly certainly she thought he didn't even have the right to defend her. But he was going to change all that.

"I'm sorry," he began. He figured that was as good a place as any to start.

"You seem to be saying that a lot lately," she commented, still looking straight ahead.

"Not enough, apparently. Look, let me take you home. Give me a chance to explain."

"After the night I had, I'm not sure I'm up to hearing your explanation."

"Fair enough. Then just let me drive you home. You don't have to listen at all. But I can get you home faster than a cab could." No response. "Besides, you haven't eaten yet. I'll go through the drive-thru at the sandwich place you like. Dinner'll be on me."

This offer at least interested her enough to earn a sidelong glance. "Will I get to eat what I want or are you going to play food cop?"

"Anything you want."

She stood up. "Fine. But I want a Philly steak sandwich, onion rings, and a shake."

"I didn't think that place sold onion rings."

"It doesn't. It doesn't sell shakes, either. You'll have to stop three times."

"Fair enough."

14

HER MOTHER had once told her a woman's purse only needed to be large enough to hold a tube of lipstick, a hundred-dollar bill, and a condom.

Why couldn't I have listened to her just that once? Things didn't get lost in small purses.

She plunged her hands into the depths of her shoulder bag, digging for her name-tag-cum-security-badge that would open the towering glass doors and let her into the station's reception area.

She glanced over her shoulder at Sam. He held five bags from three different fast-food places.

"You sure you don't want to use my badge?" He shuffled the bags to one hand and reached into his pocket.

"I've got it," she insisted, tilting her purse on its side and thrusting her hand into its depths. She rummaged for a bit and had just grasped the clip when her stapler fell out of her purse and landed square on her little toe.

"Ouch!" She hopped on one foot, clutching the injured toe of the other foot.

"Need some help?"

"No! I think you've helped enough for one night."

He swiped his badge and the door clicked open. His foot wedged between the two glass doors, he squatted to pick up her stapler. "You carry a stapler?"

She yanked it from his hands. "I like to be prepared."

His eyes meandered up the length of her body. When

his gaze met hers, his lips twitched in a smile. "I bet you made one hell of Boy Scout."

His words and tone were teasing, but there was nothing amusing about the heat of his gaze.

"Very funny." Somehow her sarcastic reply sounded strained.

Sam stood and held open the door for her. "After you...."

She glared as she walked past him into the darkened office. Overhead, every tenth light was on, providing just enough illumination for the cleaning crew and the night deejay. But the station's economic cutbacks didn't apply to the audio system. It was company policy to pipe in a live feed twenty-four, seven. From the direction of the marketing offices and the conference room came the distant murmur of a vacuum cleaner. A popular love song played on the radio and the sappy lyrics soured her mood.

She crossed the reception area trying not to favor her toe. After all, Sam had been pounded like a side of beef a couple of hours ago. If he wasn't going to limp, neither was she.

He flashed her a little half smile that went straight to her belly and made her feel all gooey inside.

Turning away, she exhaled slowly as she headed for the music room and her desk. In her haste to escape, she forgot not to limp.

She'd made it only a few steps when Sam hurried past her and dumped the bags of food onto the receptionist's counter-height desk. In a few steps he was back by her side, sweeping her up into his arms and carrying her the rest of the way to the desk.

Disoriented, she rumbled, "Put me down!"

"You're limping. You shouldn't be walking on your foot."

Instead of denying it she repeated, "Put me down before you hurt your back."

"For once let me take care of you. Besides, it wouldn't be the first time I've lifted you."

Her cheeks burned at the memory of the other times he'd held her. He'd held her when she was sick and when she was worried. He'd also held her as they'd made love.

One memory warmed her heart, the other warmed her flesh. Both made her breath catch in her throat.

He set her down, gently, on the counter. She waited for him to back away to give her enough room to hop down. He didn't. Instead he eased her shoe off to examine her toe for himself.

"It's not hurt," she protested, trying to pull her foot away.

He didn't release his hold. Cradling her stocking-clad foot in one hand, he ran his thumb across her toes. Her toes curled as a shiver ran up her leg all the way to her stomach.

She sucked air into her suddenly oxygen-deprived lungs. "Let go!"

"Stop wiggling. You could have broken something."

"I didn't."

"I can't tell anything with these hose on." He glanced up and his eyes met hers. He cocked his eyebrow. "So, tell me, Tabby, are you a panty hose or a thigh-high kind of woman?"

"What?" She tried to wiggle away, but trapped on the counter, she had nowhere to go.

Instead of answering her, he used both hands to brace her foot on his leg. His fingers traced a circle over her ankle then trailed up her calf, along the back of her knee, to her thigh. To her own amazement, she didn't object, not even when he pushed her skirt up above her knee. She couldn't resist glancing down. The lush folds of her silk dress contrasted with the sheer black of her stockings, which in turn contrasted with Sam's hands, large and strong and disappearing beneath her skirt.

Still she said nothing, but closed her eyes against the sight. It didn't matter. She felt every millimeter he touched, every spot of nylon snagged by his rough fingers. Worse still was the anticipation. Her stockings stopped mid-thigh, held in place by lacy elastic. But would he stop there? Or would he, dear God, keep searching?

Her toes clenched against his damp thigh, savoring rock-solid muscle beneath the denim of his jeans. His fingers reached the edge of her stockings, hesitated, then slipped just beyond to rest for a moment on sensitive skin. When she opened her eyes, she saw he was looking up at her, his eyes full of sensual promises. She shuddered, pressure building within her as he pressed his palms to her leg, squeezing ever so slightly. Instinctively her hips bucked off the counter, as she all but begged him to keep touching her.

Then he slipped one finger of each hand under the elastic edge of the hose, brushing against the skin. Inch by electrified inch, he rolled the stocking down, down the sensitized length of her leg, and slipped it off her foot.

She bit back a protest or maybe a groan of frustration. She wasn't sure which. Didn't know what she might say, if she allowed herself the freedom to speak.

So instead of speaking, she inhaled a deep breath, bit her tongue to keep from moaning out loud and concentrated all of her attention on not dissolving into a puddle.

One by one, he grasped each of her toes between his thumb and forefinger, massaging its length. He watched her face intently, his expression taut with desire.

Then he reached her little toe. Pain shot through her foot and she winced involuntarily. The pain was bearable, but enough to bring her back to her senses.

This time when she jerked her foot away, he let it slip from his grasp. He stepped back, giving her enough room to hop to the floor, but not enough to step away from him once she landed.

"It doesn't look broken. But you might need to ice it."

She didn't know with whom she was more annoyed—him, for his foot flirting, or herself for being so susceptible to it.

She glanced down and noticed he still held her stocking.

Him. She was definitely more annoyed at him. After all, she could still fall back on the hormonal defense. He had no excuse for his behavior.

"Give that back." She snatched the nylon and edged past him before retreating to her desk at the far end of the room.

"Hey, don't bite my head off." He followed, holding his hands up in a gesture of self-defense. "I was only trying to help."

"Right," she muttered. "Like you were trying to 'help' earlier tonight when you attacked my date?"

His easy smile faded as he cornered her by the sink. "Look, I've already apologized once. I'm not going to do it again." He brushed his fingers across her cheek, tucking a strand of hair behind her ear. "I would have done the same thing for anyone, but when I thought you were in danger... I care about you too much to..."

He stepped back, dropping his hand. She shifted under the intensity of his stare, then turned away, pressing a hand to her stomach in a vain attempt to still her unease. For a second she stared numbly at the stocking she still held, then tossed it into her bag.

"Look, you should just go." She pulled out her chair and lowered herself into it.

"I'm not going to just leave you here alone."

"I'm not alone. The cleaning staff is here and Fred's in the studio monitoring the tapes."

"Monitoring the tapes? That's a generous way of saying he's fallen asleep on top of his textbooks and won't wake up till his alarm goes off at two just in time for him to change the tape over."

Hmm. Good point. She pulled open her desk and riffled through it for a notepad. "Fred may be asleep, but he's still here."

"Regardless, he can't walk you out to your car. If whatever you're doing can't wait till morning, I'll wait."

"I'm just going to write Marty a note. Let him know what happened tonight with the date. He probably won't get it until he comes in on Monday morning, but at least he'll have some time to cool down before the ten-thirty meeting."

Sam reached over her and removed the notepad from her fingers. "I'll write the note. You're not responsible for what happened tonight." His expression suddenly grim, he said, "I am. If he's going to blame anyone, it should be me."

She raised her eyebrows. "Sam, this isn't something Marty's going to overlook. This isn't like all the times the Federal Communications Commission has fined you for inappropriate language or those times irate car-pool moms have complained about having to explain your sexual innuendos to their kids at eight in the morning. This is serious."

"Which is why he should know who was responsible."

"You? You're responsible? And I always thought you were irresponsible," she goaded him.

"Yes, I am responsible." He nodded, then his lips curved into a hint of a smile. "What? You don't think we could pin it on Jim, do you?"

"No." She couldn't help smiling back. Showing concern for her and responsibility all in one night. She was seeing a whole new side of Sam. A very adult side. "If you're doing this to impress me, it's working."

"I hoped it would."

She stood, but found Sam perilously close. Handing him the pen, she said, "While you work on this, I'll go pick up the prizes for the remote I'm working tomorrow. That way I won't have to stop by in the morning."

He nodded. "Give me five minutes, then we can walk out together."

Anticipation shivered down her spine. Then a smile teased at her lips as she said, "Try to be tactful."

"No problem. It's not the first time I've had to talk myself out of trouble with Marty."

He stepped back, giving her just enough space to pass. She felt his gaze on her as she made her way to the back hallway, which was lined on either side with two glass-fronted studios. At the end of the hall was the famed "prize closet," where Jasmine had left a selection of prizes for the remote out at the grocery store on Sunday.

She opened the door to the closet and stared into it. A mostly empty box sat on the floor and on the third shelf sat the prizes she had to choose from. Merchandize, T-shirts, and CDs. Coffee mugs, concert tickets, gift certificates. A few mandatory items were already in the box.

Normally, she'd just toss half a dozen or more items in and be done with it. But tonight, the choice seemed overwhelming.

The prize closet and the piped-in music seemed to fade. Only Sam's words remained vivid, echoing through her mind.

He cared about her. He wanted to impress her. And he was taking responsibility for what had happened.

A tiny bud of trust, which for so long had lain dormant, bloomed within her. But her natural caution snipped it back.

Unexpectedly, she thought of Newton Doyle and of the wonderful things he'd written to her. Newton, who thought she was passionate, sexy. And who'd said she was sometimes too cautious, too controlled.

Jasmine and Chandi had said essentially the same thing. These people who seemed to know her so well had seen something in her that she'd been unable to see.

"You get what you need?"

Sam's voice brought her back from her reverie.

Without turning, she stared at the shelves and shelves of merchandize. "I don't know. I don't know what I want."

For the first time in her life, she really didn't know what she wanted. Or where she was going. Or how in the world she was going to get there.

She heard Sam's footsteps approaching from behind. He rested his hand on her shoulder. "Just grab something. Whatever feels right."

That was Sam all over. A guy who grabbed whatever felt right. But also—it turned out—a guy who did the right thing. A guy who, time and again in their working relationship, had held up his end of the bargain. Done his half of the work.

And wasn't that really all she wanted in a relationship? Someone she could depend on as well as someone who could make her laugh? A blender who could make her healthy smoothies and decadent margaritas?

Wasn't that Sam?

She turned to face him. Biting down on the edge of her lip, she reached up to touch his cheek. "I think I want you."

Her words sucked his breath right out of his lungs, but it was her expression that stole his thoughts away. Hot and volatile, as if she might explode, burning them both beyond recognition. And certain. Very certain.

His world contracted to just her. Just Tabitha standing in this little corner, wanting him. And just the song playing softly in the background. Their song. "Unforgettable."

Damn it! They were at work.

He shook his head, forcing his attention to their surroundings. "Tabitha, this isn't—"

Doubt flooded her eyes. Her hand dropped to her side and she shifted away from him. "Okay. I mean, fine. I just—"

Her doubts tore at him. He needed to pull her into his arms. To hold her. To convince her that this was right. That they were right.

But this wasn't the place. Still, he didn't want to risk her pulling away from him if he waited.

He glanced back down the hall to the booth where Fred sat, head propped on his folded arms, fast asleep. Then he grabbed her arm, wrenched open the door to a nearby studio, and propelled her in, closing the door behind them. He backed her against the door, bracing a palm beside her head, forcing her to look up at him. Then he brushed his fingertips against her cheek, under her jaw, nudging her chin up so she met his gaze.

"Don't ever doubt I want you." He spoke slowly, burning the words into her mind. "Got that?"

She nodded.

"Good."

He leaned down, brushing his lips softly against hers. Her eyes closed in anticipation of the onslaught to come. He kissed her once, twice, three times. With each pass, he tried to pull back, but the seductive rhythm of the music and the irresistible pulsing of desire urged him on in maddening increments.

"Sam?"

"Yeah?" Another delicate kiss, but this time his hand dropped to her shoulder to toy with the strap of her dress.

"Why aren't you kissing me?"

He smiled at the frustration in her voice. "I thought I was."

"Stop teasing me."

"Tabitha, this isn't the place."

"I don't care." She gasped, arching against him. "We're alone here. I want you."

Her words propelled desire through his body, to his very soul. The need to possess her, to abandon caution, to drive her over the edge, thundered through his veins.

Everything had happened too quickly last time. She'd regretted it and he didn't want that to happen again.

"Tabitha—"

"Sam, please."

This time there would be no regrets—for either of them. She arched against him and her kiss stole his breath away. Robbed him, not only of his breath, but also of thought and restraint. The instant he felt her tongue sliding across his, he lost it all. And gained something else in return. Oxygen, logic, strength of will were all nothing compared to the heady passion of having her in his arms.

Only one thing surpassed the sweet victory of feeling her lose control, and that was knowing she hadn't lost it too soon. He'd seen the awareness in her eyes, seen the knowledge. This act, this passion, this kiss—they were no hormonal glitch.

She'd never be able to talk herself out it, never be able to turn her back on what was happening here or to turn her back on him. For now, for tonight, and maybe for forever, she was his. Truly and completely his.

He bathed her in kisses, immersing himself in the feel and taste of her—her hair, her skin, her breath. He kissed her everywhere, as if he could absorb her essence through his lips, lavishing attention on spots he'd never thought to before—the crook of her elbow and the inside of her wrist, the back of her knee and the small of her back. Finally, when he smoothed the dampened silk of her dress and brought her nipple into his mouth, she was almost as crazy with desire as he was.

The dress, damp where it had touched him, clung to her body, delineated every curve, every dip, every slope. Like a modern incarnation of some ancient goddess, she was rounded, smooth yet ripe, and she brought him to his knees.

He knelt in front of her and, for a moment, his hand hovered above the swollen mound of her belly, trembling. He closed his eyes and rested his cheek against her stomach. Only when he felt her hands shifting through his hair did he raise his head. The sight of her half-open eyes, moist, parted lips and flushed skin brought a smile to his lips.

For the second time that night he eased his hands under her slip. This time he did what he'd only fantasized about before. He slid his hands under the elastic edging of her panties, his fingers relishing the rounded flesh of her buttocks, his thumbs teasing the delicate skin just inside her hips, before gently pulling the scrap of silk from her body.

He moved her back onto the stretch of counter lining the wall, lifting her until she perched on the edge. Then he spread her knees, running his hands up the length of her creamy thighs, his lips following in the wake of his fingertips. He savored every aspect of her reaction, every shiver, every gasp, every convulsion.

She pulled him to her, wrapping her legs around his waist, gasping out a need echoed by his own. Yet, still he pushed, relentless in his determination to drive her over the edge. He wanted her to lose herself so completely he would be her only path home.

15

BY MORNING, guilt and confusion were gnawing through her. Even Sam's embrace—as comfortable and worn in as a favorite pair of ten-year-old jeans—couldn't sooth her churning emotions.

Yes, being in Sam's arms felt right—so right she couldn't help wonder why she hadn't been doing it for years. And yes, she loved him. Loving Sam had snuck up on her so quietly and swiftly she hadn't even realized it was happening.

Yet, despite all that—or perhaps because of it—her doubts haunted her. No matter how much she loved Sam, there was a tiny part of her heart he could never touch. The part that belonged to Newton Doyle. A man whose face she'd never seen, whose voice she'd never heard. Whose touch she'd never felt. But he was as real to her as the man who'd spent most of the night beside her. Because with Newton she felt as if she'd seen and heard and felt his very soul.

But she'd made her choice and made it with her eyes open. Last night when she'd made love with Sam, she'd allowed him into her body and her heart.

She didn't regret it. But she did regret the pain she may have caused Newton. He'd done nothing but help her, and she was fairly certain she was going to hurt him. If she'd opened her heart to him, then he'd done the same for her.

Without his words, she wouldn't have had the courage to open her heart to Sam. Newton had told her to take a risk. He'd encouraged her to be less cautious. She'd followed his advice and it had led her into the arms of another man.

At the very least, she needed to see him—to meet him once in person—and to try to explain.

While Sam had been with her, his presence had held her reservations at bay. But after he left her in the early morning, the void left by his absence was quickly filled by her doubts.

So, the next morning, with a knotted stomach and a heavy heart, she opened her dresser drawer and slipped her hand under her clothes to find the thin envelope that held Newton Doyle's first letter.

She'd stared at the return address printed in the upper left-hand corner so often, the numbers and street blurred together. Like a commonly misspelled word, it seemed familiar but somehow wrong.

Her Mapsco showed her the street was in Clarksville, one of the many once rundown but now revitalized residential neighborhoods near downtown Austin.

As she drove through the near-empty streets of the warehouse district on her way to Clarksville, she speculated about the more mundane aspects of Newton Doyle. Either he lived in one of the unrenovated dumps or a decade ago he'd had the foresight to invest in what was then iffy real estate. Or maybe he was one of the new Austinites just willing to pay outrageous rent for a trendy address.

She found herself hoping he was the latter. She didn't want to like Newton Doyle any more than she already did. If Newton Doyle was a vain, self-indulgent rich guy who just happened to have a nice turn of phrase, that was okay by her. If in person, he was as sensitive and insightful as he was in writing, that would only make telling him goodbye harder. But she would still do it.

She turned onto his block, her gaze skipping to the far end where his house, 124-B, was located. The "B" probably meant he lived in one half of a duplex or an apartment, since many of the turn-of-the-century foursquare houses had later been split into smaller units.

As she eased to a stop in front of his house just behind a gleaming new Volkswagen, her gut churned with repressed longing and unrepressed guilt, not a good mixture on an empty stomach. She pressed her palm to her abdomen to quell her nerves and thought of the baby nestled within. And she thought of Sam, who'd been so unexpectedly supportive throughout her pregnancy.

She'd made the right choice. Whatever else happened between the two of them, she trusted him. He would never hurt her baby and he would never hurt her.

That thought alone gave her the strength to open her car door and make her way up the worn concrete stairs to the columned front porch of the aging but lovingly maintained Victorian house. Two front doors opened onto the porch at ninety-degree angles to each other, a dulled brass "A" and "B" nailed to each. Just below the B was a nameplate with Newton's name and address, probably to avoid confusion since the two doors of the duplex were so close.

Her breath quivered through her lungs as she pressed the ringer just below the B. She waited.

Seconds and then minutes crawled by. She glanced at her watch. Ten-thirty. Surely early enough for most people to be up and moving on a Sunday morning—people who hadn't had their Saturday nights disrupted by lakeside brawls and earth-shattering sex.

She rang the bell again, standing on her toes in a vain attempt to see into the narrow window at the top of the door. Finally she heard footsteps approaching. Then the turning of a lock.

She had the ridiculous sensation that her life hung in balance, that the next few minutes would change its course. And it did.

Just as the door swung open, she tilted her head and looked at the nameplate under door A.

The wood floorboards of the porch tilted out from under her as she read the name: Sam Stevens.

"Hey, man, are you okay?"

Unable to take her eyes from the name on the brass plate, she swayed, then felt a hand grab her arm to steady her. Moving as if in slow motion, she turned her eyes first to the hand, then up the arms to the shoulder, and finally to the face. Her breath felt trapped in her throat, unable to reach her lungs as she looked into the eyes of Newton Doyle for the first time.

She recognized him instantly. He was the man she'd seen Sam talking to at the 5-K Run. His appearance was too distinct for there to be any doubt. He was not just some listener. He was Sam's neighbor. Sam's friend.

The hand around her arm tightened. "Tabitha, you all right?"

"Yes." No. Dear God, no. She squeezed her eyes tightly shut. Then she forced them open. "You're Newton Doyle."

"Yeah. I'm Newt." He strained to look around her toward Sam's door, no doubt trying to figure out what, if anything, Sam had to do with her presence.

"You look really...you know, not...good. Do you need to sit down or something?"

"I'll be fine," she said, peeling his fingers from around

her arm. But without his support, she still felt woozy, so she braced her hand on his door frame. "You're the one who sent the letters. The letters Sam wrote."

She was stating the obvious. This man—more of a boy, really—clearly didn't have the verbal skills or the insight to have communicated with her the way the man from the letters had. But Sam did.

Newton—no, Newt—blushed and looked nervously toward Sam's door. "Um, maybe I should, you know, get Sam. I think maybe you should talk to him."

Finally her world righted itself as anger flared to life within her. "Talk to Sam? Oh, I will most definitely be talking to Sam about this. But before I do, I just want to know one thing. Why? Why did he do this?"

She couldn't begin to comprehend why the man she trusted...the man she'd thought she loved...would manipulate her in this childish fashion.

Newt shifted nervously from foot to foot. Once again he looked beyond her, no doubt hoping the cavalry would ride up and rescue him from her questioning.

"Well, you see, I'd written the program. But it didn't work. And Sam was like 'there's no way she'll dig this.' And Sam's such a great guy he wrote the first letter for me. But he really wanted me to meet you and go out with you. But I'm totally, like, not good with women."

Finally his gaze shifted to her face. His mouth dropped open at her expression. "But I guess you can tell that, huh?"

"So the letters, the e-mails, those were all Sam?"

"Well, yeah, I guess. He used my computer. But he wrote them. Later, I tried to tell him to tell you, but I guess he never got around to it."

He never got around to it?

He'd signed someone else's name.

He'd written her letters she'd fallen in love with, but he'd never gotten around to telling her. Why?

Newt, fount of information that he was, couldn't give her the answers. Only Sam could do that.

She turned ninety degrees to stare at Sam's door. Somewhere, mere feet away, Sam lay sleeping in bed. She briefly considered pounding on the door, demanding answers.

But emotion—anger, doubt and grief—welled up inside of her, prickling the backs of her eyes and clutching her throat. In that instant she wanted nothing more than to sink to the ground, curl into a ball and cry. She needed solitude far more than she needed answers.

So without even looking at Newton Doyle, she walked back down the porch's front steps to her car. Newt watched her the whole way, but she was barely aware of his scrutiny.

By the time she climbed into her car, the clock in her dash read ten forty-seven. She had thirteen minutes to make it to the grocery store in South Austin where Jasmine was already working the remote. She drove there mindlessly, thinking only of Sam and what her discovery meant to their relationship.

She could think of just three reasons why Sam had written the letters to her. One, he'd been secretly in love with her all along. But if that were the case, why use Newton's name instead of making one up? Especially since Newton clearly had expected to meet her. Two, he'd done it just to help out his friend. Frankly, she just didn't think Sam was that nice of a guy. Three, he'd seen it as a way of boosting ratings.

She didn't like option three. Just the thought made her feel as though a huge fist was squeezing her heart. But it was the most logical. Sam had said it himself, without good ratings they didn't have jobs. And she knew how important his job was to him.

The only question was, where did this leave her emotionally? And what did it say about their relationship?

Had it been nothing more than an act on his part?

She couldn't believe that. He'd been too passionate. Too "into her," as Jasmine would say. The attraction between them had been building for years. It simply could not have been faked.

Then it hit her. Both times they'd been together, she'd all but begged him to make love to her. Both times, she'd been the initiator. True, he'd been the first to kiss her, but when it came to the deed itself, she'd been calling the shots.

Yes, the attraction had been there all along, but she'd pushed their relationship to the next level. And in doing so, she may have mistaken passion for something entirely more meaningful.

If she got hurt, she had no one to blame but herself.

SHE WAS LATE showing up at the remote. After parking her car at the far end of the parking lot, she made her way toward the K-O-N-E tent and van, from which one of the deejays was broadcasting live. She felt like a burn victim; exposed, raw and dazed.

Jasmine didn't notice her state or her lateness. As soon as Tabitha reached the tent and set down her box of prizes she'd barely remembered to bring home last night, the other woman pulled her to a back corner, out of the range of the stray customers wandering by, and whispered, "Did you hear about what happened last night?"

It took a full second for Tabitha to realize Jasmine must be referring to the debacle at the lake. She feigned nonchalance. "Of course. I was there. It was a nightmare. But luckily the police got it all sorted out pretty quickly."

Jasmine frowned, confusion written clearly across her face. "It was you? Wow, you're the last person I'd have thought. But the police? What were they doing there?" Then her eyes widened. "Don't tell me it was a group thing! That's so kinky."

"It was weird, but I don't know that I'd call it kinky." Tabitha dug through her purse for a pair of sunglasses to shield her eyes from the glare off the parking lot and to shield her soul from Jasmine's prying eyes. Then she moved away to tuck her purse behind the curtained legs of the table. "But of course the police came. Sam insisted. He nearly had my date arrested."

"Huh?" Jasmine flopped into one of the folding chairs. "What are you talking about?"

"I'm talking about what happened last night with my date. Sam thought he was one of 'America's Most Dangerous Criminals' and tried to make a citizen's arrest. What are you talking about?"

"Oh, that." Jasmine dismissed it with a wave of her hand. "That's old news."

"Old news? It happened just last night." Okay, so it was ridiculous—especially given the current state of her emotional health—to be arguing that Jasmine should pay more attention to an event that Tabitha hoped everyone would just forget. But still, the end results had been earth-shattering. "Never mind. Forget it."

"Don't you want to hear the new news?"

"You, apparently, want to tell me."

"Last night, long after Sam's little dip in Town Lake, someone snuck into the station. They had sex in one of the studios."

"Oh, my God." The prayer escaped from Tabitha's

lips. The blood drained from her face, but Jasmine didn't seem to notice.

"I know!" Jasmine's gaze darted in either direction and she leaned forward, clearly thrilled to be sharing such salacious gossip.

"How did you find out?" Tabitha asked. "Did Fred say something?"

"No. Fred was asleep. You know him, the guy's like a narcoleptic or something."

"Then who? The cleaning staff."

"No, much worse. Here's the kicker. The mike was on."

"What?" Tabitha jumped to her feet. "Are you sure?"

"Absolutely. Someone did the nasty in one of the studios and all of Austin heard." Jasmine sat back and crossed her legs. "Well, it was sometime around midnight, so technically only about point two percent of Austin was listening but, still, pretty wild, huh?"

The energy that had propelled Tabitha to her feet left just as quickly. She sank back into her chair, numb with humiliation and shock. "Unbelievable."

"I know."

"How could this happen?" She hadn't meant to ask the question out loud.

Nevertheless, Jasmine answered. "Well, I stopped by the station this morning. That's how I heard about it."

"Does everyone know?"

"No, only a few people. Marty's there, absolutely having fits."

"Marty knows?"

"Yeah, some friend of his who listens online in Australia called him late last night. Anyway, he's up at the station trying to sort things out. At first he thought it was just someone acting out a fantasy of doing it on the air.

But then he realized the mike was still on in that booth. He thinks one of the cleaning crew accidentally switched it on."

Tabitha leaned forward and buried her head in her hands. She'd spent her whole life being so responsible, so careful. Now, one by one, the carefully placed bricks that made up her life were crumbling in front of her eyes. And there didn't seem to be a damn thing she could do to stop it.

First the baby, then her affair with Sam, then her job at the station. Bam, bam, bam. Goodbye emotional and financial security. Goodbye retirement fund.

And yet...did she really regret anything that had happened?

She never would have chosen single motherhood, but she already loved the baby. She couldn't regret becoming pregnant.

Falling in love with Sam probably wasn't the smartest thing she'd ever done, especially in light of what she'd learned this morning. But with Sam, for the first time in her entire life, she'd taken risks. Not crossing-the-street-on-the Don't Walk little risks, either, but full-blown, jump-off-a-cliff-without-a-parachute risks. And she'd survived, stronger than ever. Loving Sam had taught her her own strength. And job or no job, she'd never be the same again.

So she couldn't, in all fairness, regret that, either. In the past few weeks her life had taken dramatic turns, but she'd do it all over again if she had the choice.

Of course, she hadn't really absorbed the enormity of the events. Maybe that's why she suddenly felt eerily calm.

Thinking out loud, she said, "If Marty finds out who it was, they'll be fired."

Jasmine, unaware of Tabitha's inner turmoil, nodded sagely. "Yep. He's working on it already. But he can't really learn anything until this afternoon at the earliest."

"Why not?"

"He's already called in Neil, the guy who designed the security system, but Neil can't make it in until then. Apparently, it'll be pretty simple to dig into the system and track the badges for that day. Once they know who went in, they'll have the guy."

Sam. They'd have Sam.

Tabitha's heart sank.

Last night they'd entered the studio using his badge because she couldn't find hers.

She was more than willing to accept the consequences of her actions, but now her mistakes would end up costing both of them their jobs. That she wouldn't stand for.

Somehow it didn't matter that Sam had betrayed her trust. It didn't matter that he'd hurt her. She still loved him—loved him enough to sacrifice her job for his.

But she had to get to the station before Neil did.

She stood abruptly, then squatted to grab her purse from under the table. "I've got to go."

"What? You just got here!"

"I know, I'm sorry. But I have to go talk to Marty. It's an emergency." She scanned the parking lot. "I'm sorry to leave you here alone, but it doesn't seem that busy today anyway."

Jasmine stood, concern written clearly on her face. "Okay. Sure I can handle it." She ran her hands over her spiky hair as if prepping herself for the onslaught of people who would approach the table over the next several hours. "I'll see you Monday then."

Tabitha almost left it at that. But Jasmine was too close a friend. By Monday the station would be alive with gossip, and when Jasmine heard the news from someone else, her feelings would be hurt.

She placed a hand on Jasmine's arm. "No, you probably won't see me on Monday. I was the one at the studio last night."

"What?" Jasmine's voice rose several octaves. "You?"

Before Jasmine could start digging, Tabitha fabricated a lie that she hoped would hold water. "Yes. After the date last night, Sam drove me back to the station. I didn't have my key, so he used his to let me in. Then he left. I called Bob to come pick me up, and one thing led to another."

"Bob? You're back with Bob?"

"No." She'd never be back with Bob. Poor toaster oven that he was, he'd never live up to the memories of a blender. "It was just a one-night stand. A mistake."

That one word summed up so much that had happened in the past few weeks. But sometimes mistakes turned out for the best.

16

"WHERE'S TABITHA? I need to see her." Sam elbowed his way past a couple of teenage girls and a balding middle-aged man to reach the K-O-N-E table.

Jasmine, looking as deflated as a kid who'd just had her stash of candy stolen, didn't even look up. She was listlessly handing out the entry forms for the drawings that would be held throughout the day.

"She's not here." When she looked up at Sam, her eyes filled with tears. "You two would have been so good together. Why didn't it work out?"

He felt as if he'd been punched in the gut.

Why indeed? He'd been asking himself that same question ever since Newt had woken him a half hour ago and told him what had happened. Why hadn't he just told her last night?

He'd never thought she'd go visit Newt this morning, that's why. He thought he had plenty of time. Since she'd be working all afternoon, he'd envisioned spending the time hitting a few of the local jewelry stores to look for engagement rings. Then Newt had barged in and turned his world upside down.

Now he had to find Tabitha and explain. She probably thought the worst, and he couldn't blame her. But he could explain. He could fix it, if only he could find her.

"Look," he said to Jasmine, "I know I screwed up. But I can fix it. I just need to know where she is."

"No, Sam. I don't think you can fix it."

He listened in confusion and growing shock as Jasmine explained everything that had happened. By the time Jasmine was done, he'd sunk to the folding chair and buried his head in his hands.

God, what a mess.

When he finally looked up, it was to see Jasmine—as well as a small circle of bystanders—watching him. "Bob?" he asked numbly. "She said she was up there with Bob?"

Jasmine shrugged. "That's what she said."

"And you believed her?"

She stiffened, indignation delineating her features. "Tabitha wouldn't lie."

He sighed. "Of course Tabitha would lie. She'd lie to protect someone she loved." She had lied to protect him.

But why hadn't she just come home and discussed it with him? Why hadn't she trusted that together they would figure this out? If they went to Marty together, surely they could work something out. Why hadn't she seen it?

What did you think, genius? That'd she'd trust you after she found out you'd lied to her?

So why take the blame for it herself?

Because she was Tabitha, strong and brave, and still trying to control everything. Still trying to be the responsible one.

Damn it, it was time he proved to her once and for all that he could protect her. That he loved her. And that he was worthy of her love.

He stood and pulled his cell phone out of his back pocket. After punching the first several digits of Marty's office number, he realized his phone wasn't working—thanks to its dip in the lake.

Tossing it aside, he asked Jasmine, "Can I borrow your phone?"

"Sure." Her confused expression didn't fade as she dug through her purse and pulled it out. "What are you going to do?"

"I'm going to stop Tabitha from making a big mistake."

Again he punched in the numbers, then waited restlessly for the call to go through. The phone rang, but Marty didn't pick up. He tried Tabitha's cell phone next, but she didn't answer, either.

His fingers itched to hurl the useless phone across the parking lot, but instead he handed it back to Jasmine. "How long ago did she leave?"

"Just a few minutes before you got here."

If he left now, could he make it to the station before she did? Only if he was planning on flying there.

Damn it, there had to be a way he could talk to her before she got to the station and ruined her career.

He paced the length of the tent, then turned and paced back. Across the edges of his consciousness drifted the latest U2 ballad, which played softly in the background from the speakers set up on the corners of the tent.

Finally he turned back to Jasmine. "Tabitha listens to our station in the car, right?"

She nodded, still confused. "Sure, but why?"

"Let's just hope she's listening today."

STOPPED AT A LIGHT, half a mile from the station, Tabitha reached over to turn off the radio. She'd been listening to it for the past ten minutes, trying to block out her own thoughts on the drive to the station. It wasn't working.

Her hand was already on the dial when the song ended and she heard a voice that made her breath catch in her throat.

"Hope y'all don't mind, but I'm going to steal a little air time," Sam's voice said.

She stared in shock at her car radio. Either she was hallucinating, or her car was possessed, or Sam was about to do something very stupid.

The car behind her honked. She looked up and realized the light had changed to green. Mindlessly she turned into a nearby parking lot and shifted into park, all her concentration still focused on Sam's voice.

"Tabitha, honey, I sure hope you're listening 'cause I have a letter here I want to read to you. By now you know I've been sending you letters under another name as part of the station's Love Letters To Tabitha contest. You probably think I was doing it to increase the ratings or something stupid like that, but I wasn't.

"The truth is, Tabitha, I'm in love with you."

Tabitha swallowed hard, unsuccessfully trying to blink away her tears. "Oh, Sam."

"These past couple of weeks, listening to the letters other men have sent you and knowing you were going to go out with one of them, it's about killed me. I don't want you to go out with anyone else. I want you to be with me. I want us—all of us—to be a family.

"Now you probably don't believe me, so I've a got another letter to read to you. This one I wrote as myself. It's from me to you, and I want everyone to hear it."

Through the radio, she heard the faint rustling of paper, as if he really was pulling out a letter he'd written.

Then he read, "'Dear Tabitha... The mornings don't last long enough anymore. Long after you've gone home for the day and your voice has been replaced by the latest pop song, I find myself missing you.

"'Sometimes, I turn on the radio during the day just to hear you read the ads. And for the first time in my life, I want to hear less music and more commercials. Except when it comes to that jazzed up version of "Unforgettable." It's our song, Tabitha. I hear it and I think of you. I think of us.

"'But it's not enough anymore. I need more than just your mornings now. I need your afternoons, your evenings and your nights. I need to fall asleep with you in my arms and wake up beside you. I need you.'

"That's the letter I was going to give you today, Tabitha. If you'll come back to me, you'll see that I mean it. You'll see that I signed it myself. I should have given you the letter last night, after we left the station, but I wanted to wait until today when I could give you the letter and an engagement ring."

She gasped at his words, then bit down on her lip. He was going to ask her to marry him? Sam? Commitment-phobe Sam had just asked her to marry him on the radio?

Then the rest of what he'd said sunk in. Not only did he love her, not only was he going to tell her about the letters from Newt, but he'd also just admitted to being at the station last night.

Most of the listening audience wouldn't make the connection, but Marty surely would. Here she'd been about to sacrifice her career for his, and he'd beaten her to the punch. Even if she'd doubted what he'd said over the radio, that was undeniable proof that he really did love her.

She slipped her car into gear and headed back to the grocery store, where the station had been broadcasting live and where Sam was sure to be.

She made it to the grocery store in half the time. After

reading the letter Sam had cued up "Unforgettable." The last notes of the song were just fading as she pulled into the parking lot.

Climbing out of her car, she saw him standing in front of the tent. A crowd of about twenty people had gathered around him. He stood there, boots planted firmly on the ground, wearing jeans and an untucked, unbuttoned shirt over a white T-shirt.

As she crossed the parking lot, a murmur ran through the crowd. A second later he turned and spotted her. The crowd parted and she realized his white shirt bore the words 'I ♥ Tabitha.'

Despite the tears in her eyes, she smiled. He met her halfway across the parking lot.

She wanted to throw herself into his arms, but he held her face in his hands and studied her. Without saying a word he lowered his mouth to hers.

His lips, warm and moist, coaxed hers open in an intimate greeting. His mouth covered hers in a slow exploration, as if testing her emotional state without asking outright.

Not wanting him to have any doubt about her answer, she wrapped her arms around him and kissed him back. He relaxed into her embrace, home at last.

Over the thrumming of her heart she heard the applause and cheers of the small crowd gathered around the tent.

When he finally pulled back, he asked, "So what do you say?"

Looking up at him, she couldn't help teasing. "First, I want my letter."

He pulled the sheet of paper from his breast pocket and handed it to her. She carefully unfolded the page. Unlike the other letter from Newton, this one was handwritten on lined paper torn from a spiral notebook. How perfectly Sam.

"And second?" he asked, one eyebrow quirked.

"Second, I want to know why you're wearing that awful 'I ♥ Tabitha' T-shirt."

His lips spread into a full smile. "I figured this would have to be my new lucky T-shirt. You've still got my other one." He ran a fingertip across her jawline. "So, what do you say, Tabby. Wanna get married?" Then his other hand drifted to her hip where his thumb traced a lazy circle. "Wanna make me a dad?"

Her heart expanded in her chest to the point she thought it might explode. "Yes, yes, I do."

He kissed her again, and when he pulled back, she added, "I don't know how we're going to live, since I'm pretty sure we're both out of a job now."

"Nah," he murmured. "Marty's not gonna fire us. I just proposed on live radio. By tomorrow morning the whole town will tune in to hear whether or not you accepted. Marty would be a fool not to take advantage of that. And Marty's no fool."

"You're right," she mused, twining her fingers together behind his back to pull him even closer. "Funny, I'm not as relieved as I thought I'd be to still have a job." She tilted her head to look up at him. "I guess I'm just glad to still have you. You know what I mean?"

He chuckled. "Hell, yes."

Pressing his forehead to hers, he gazed deeply into her eyes. The glistening of tears she saw there took her breath away.

"After Newt talked to me this morning, I was sure I'd lost you forever."

"About Newt..." She almost told him everything she'd felt when she'd learned the truth about Newton Doyle's letters, but stopped herself. There'd be time for that later. For now she just wanted to relish in the feel of his arms around her.

"Yeah?" The caution in his voice got to her.

"The old house in Clarksville? That's yours, isn't it?"

"Yeah. What about it?"

"I'm just surprised, that's all."

"I bought it years ago. I knew it'd be a good investment." His hands tightened on her hips. "And I think part of me was hoping someday I'd find someone who wanted to live with me there. You want to kick Newt out and turn it from a duplex into a home for us?"

She laughed. "After all these years, I find out that Wild Man Sam is a smart investor who secretly wants to settle down. Is there anything else I don't know about you?"

"I don't think you know how much I love you."

Epilogue

"I'M TELLING YOU, FOLKS, sometimes you can see love coming from miles away. Sometimes you don't see it until after it's blindsided you." Sam spoke the words into his cell phone, but his attention was firmly held by the woman who lay in the hospital bed, a child in her arms. He stood just outside her hospital room, unwilling to disturb her as she nursed their daughter.

On the other end of the line, Jasmine—who'd taken over the morning show while he and Tabitha were on leave—was patching the call through to the radio.

"With a newborn baby, it's a little bit of both. You know you're going to love her, but you're never prepared for how much." His throat tightened around the words. He swallowed hard before continuing. "Tabitha and I want to thank everyone who sent cards, flowers and gifts. We really appreciate it. I'll be back on the air next Monday. Y'all go easy on Jasmine and don't have too much fun without me."

A few seconds later he snapped the phone closed and slipped it into his shirt pocket. Tabitha looked up as he silently came through the door.

"She's a hungry little thing."

Sam lowered himself to the edge of the bed. "Is she demanding an Oreo cookie with her milk yet?"

Tabitha smiled, her eyes lighting with mischief. "No, not yet. I could use an Oreo cookie, though, if you're offering to run out and get me one."

Oreo cookies had become their little joke. Partly because she'd eaten so many of them during her pregnancy, but mostly because they were part of the first gift he'd ever given her. "Hmm, the hospital gift shop didn't have any. I did get little Samantha here a gift, though." He held out the gift-shop bag.

Tabitha shifted Samantha in her arms and extracted the tiny 'I ♥ Mommy' T-shirt. She laughed, shaking her head. "Sam..."

"Hey," he shrugged, "it matches mine." Despite her protests, he often wore his lucky 'I ♥ Tabitha' T-shirt.

She rolled her eyes, but her smile told him she loved it. His heart tightened. As he'd said on the radio, falling in love with Tabitha had blindsided him. But now he couldn't imagine life without her and couldn't imagine why he'd fought it for so long.

With a reverent hand, he brushed a fine lock of ebony hair from his daughter's forehead. And there was no doubt she was his daughter. In his mind and his heart, biology had nothing to do with it. She was as much his as her mother was.

A tiny version of Tabitha, Samantha had black hair, already long enough to show it had curl, and a baby's blue eyes that he knew one day would sharpen to the china-blue of Tabitha's.

She was so tiny, so delicate, his heart ached just looking at her. He ran a finger down her arm to her fat little fist. Her delicate fingers opened then closed over his forefinger.

No doubt about it, she already had him wrapped around her little finger. Just like her mother.

When Suzanne, Nicole and Taylor vow to stay single, they don't count on meeting these sexy bachelors!

ROUGHING IT WITH RYAN
January 2003

TANGLING WITH TY
February 2003

MESSING WITH MAC
March 2003

Don't miss this sexy new miniseries by Jill Shalvis—
one of Temptation's hottest authors!

Available at your favorite retail outlet.

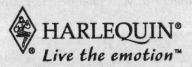

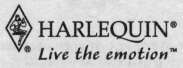

HARLEQUIN®
Temptation

COMING NEXT MONTH